W9-AHY-794
Mill Valley Middle School
Library
240839

The Dragon's Son

The Dragon's Son

by Sarah L. Thomson

ORCHARD BOOKS ~ NEW YORK
An Imprint of Scholastic Inc.

Orchard Books
An Imprint of Scholastic Inc.
95 Madison Avenue
New York, NY 10016

Manufactured in the United States of America
Book design by Rosanne Kakos-Main
The text of this book is set in 11.5 point Cochin.
10 9 8 7 6 5 4 3 2 1

Library of Congress Cataloging-in-Publication Data
Thomson, Sarah L.
The dragon's son / by Sarah L. Thomson
p. cm.
Summary: Based on the Mabinogion, a collection of medieval Welsh tales, as well as later legends, and tells of family members and servants important in the life of King Arthur, featuring Nimue, Morgan le Fay, Luned, and Mordred.
ISBN 0-531-30333-0 (alk. paper)
1. Lady of the Lake (legendary character)—Juvenile fiction. 2. Morgan le Fay (legendary character)—Juvenile fiction. 3. Luned (legendary character)—Juvenile fiction. 4. Mordred (legendary character)—Juvenile fiction. [1. Lady of the Lake (legendary character)—Fiction. 2. Morgan le Fay (legendary character)—Fiction. 3. Luned (legendary character)—Fiction. 4. Mordred (legendary character)—Fiction. 5. Arthur, King—Fiction. 6. Great Britain—History—To 1066—Fiction.] I. Title.
PZ7.T378 Dr 2001 [Fic]—dc21 00-61177

For my parents
and in loving memory of
Paul and Grace James
and
Whitey and Emma Thomson

Author's Note

IT'S A.D. 500 IN THE ISLAND OF BRITAIN.

Ninety years ago—almost four generations—this was a distant outpost of the Roman Empire. Roman governors ruled the country, and many people lived in great Roman cities like Bath and London. They traveled on Roman roads, paid Roman taxes in Roman coin. Some of them spoke Latin. They were protected by Roman legions from the armed raiding parties that came from Ireland or from the parts of Britain where Roman rule didn't reach.

But when the Roman Empire began to crumble, Rome withdrew troops and officials from distant colonies like Britain. By A.D. 410, Britain was no longer a Roman colony.

Now, in A.D. 500, small British kingdoms have grown up to replace the Roman government. These kingdoms face threats from all sides: from the Irish, from the Picts—a Roman term for the people from the north of Britain, what will later be called Scotland—and from their own neighbors. Civil war is as common, and as devastating, as attacks from the outside. There is also a new enemy: Germanic tribes from the north of Europe, often lumped together under the name of Saxons. Many of them have already settled in the south and east of Britain, and they continue to push their way westward. The British kingdoms have been steadily losing ground to them.

Archeological evidence suggests that sometime around the late fifth or early sixth century this trend was temporarily reversed. For a brief period—not much longer than a generation—the Saxons halted their westward advance. When early British historians wrote of this time, they described a powerful leader who defeated the Germanic invaders and created a brief haven of peace amid the chaos. Later writers gave this leader a name: Arthur.

Almost nothing else is known about this military hero. It was long afterward that storytellers and poets created an entire cycle of stories around King Arthur, stories not only of military success but of love, friendship, and betrayal; of chivalry and quests; of magic and mystery.

In retelling this story of Arthur, I found myself drawn to the earliest surviving stories about him. These are medieval Welsh tales, and they lack several parts of the Arthurian story that modern readers are familiar with: the quest for the grail; the adultery between Arthur's queen and his best friend; the treachery of Mordred, Arthur's nephew-son. But the Welsh tales have several interesting characters who have dropped out of the later retellings: Gwenhwyfach, the queen's sister; Owain ap Urien, who commanded an army of ravens; Luned, the servant who could manage things so much better than her lady.

Drawn by these tantalizing hints of ancient tales, I began to imagine a story of Arthur that would look back to the original roots of the legend and also harmonize with later retellings, particularly Thomas Malory's epic *Le Morte D'Arthur*, written in the fifteenth century. I also found that I wanted to give a voice to characters who don't often get to speak for themselves, characters like Nimue, Morgan, and Mordred. To find out why these people behaved the way they did, I had to imagine stories.

Whatever the historical background, the legend of King Arthur has lasted centuries simply because it's a good story—of the conflicts of ideals, of love and betrayal, of the desperate attachments and hopeless divisions between human beings. Like all good stories, it invites endless telling and retelling. To ask whether King Arthur really existed may intrigue historians and archeologists, but for writers and readers of fiction, it's the wrong question. The *stories* exist, endlessly varied, different in every age. More than enough.

Pronunciation of Names

any of the characters' names in *The Dragon's Son* come from Welsh stories and poems, which are the oldest written sources for the King Arthur legends. Most of the letters are pronounced more or less as in English, with some exceptions. A few hints:

C and *g* are always hard (like *car* and *garden*, not *circle* and *George*).
Ch is a back-of-the-throat sound, like the *ch* in the Scottish *loch*.
Dd is pronounced like the English *th* in *then*.
F is pronounced like the English *v*.
A single *l* is like the English *l*.
Ll is unique to Welsh; it is pronounced by putting the tip of your tongue on the front teeth and blowing around it. If you can't manage this, pronounce *ll* like *tl* and you'll be fairly close.
W and *y* are considered vowels in Welsh.
The word *ap*, as in "Arthur ap Uther," means "son of.

These names should be pronounced as follows:

Alun: AHL-un
Angharad: Ahng-HAR-ahd
Baedan: BY-dahn
Bran: BRAHN
Branwen: BRAHN-wen
Bedwyr: BED-wur

Caerleon: kire-LAY-on
Cafall: KAHV-ahll
Cawdor: COW-dore
Cei: KAY
Cigfa: KIG-vah
Cynan: CUN-en
Dafydd: DAHV-ith
Duach: DOO-ach
Dylan: DULL-en
Gawain: GAH-wen
Gereint: GER-aint
Goewin: GOY-win
Gormant: GOR-mant
Gwenhwyfach: gwen-HWIH-vach
Gwenhwyfar: gwen-HWIH-var
Gwenllian: gwen-LLEE-ahn
Gwydre: GWID-ray
Gwyn: GWIN
Gwythr: GWIH-thur
Hafgan: HAHV-gahn
Hywel: HUH-wel
Lleu: LLEE
Luned: LEEN-ed
Medraud: MED-rawd
Meilyr: MAY-lur
Morfudd: MOHR-vith
Myrddin: MUR-thin
Nimue: NIM-oo-eh
Nudd: NEETH
Olwen: OHL-wen
Owain: OH-wen
Rheged: RHAY-ged
Rhian: RHEE-ahn
Rhiogan: RYE-o-gan
Siawn: SHAWN
Sinnoch: SHEEN-och
Tannwen: TAHN-wen
Uther: OO-thur

Nimue

Y FATHER WAS A FERRYMAN. I grew up by the river, learning by heart her moods and whims, her quiet songs. I knew her birds by the flash of their wings in the reeds, knew where her fish hid in deep, quiet pools. I could wander all day along her banks and she would always lie there, like a silver string behind me, to lead me home in the dusk.

Every time I had to turn around I wished I could keep walking, following her waters to places far beyond our tiny village. Places where there were courts and kings and warriors, cities of stone, merchants, foreign traders with their strange tongues and strangers' faces—everything in the stories told by the travelers who came to cross the water.

But year after year the travelers came and went and I stayed in the little house by the river, cooking for my father, sewing and weaving, catching fish for dinner. Sometimes I'd let a silver trout wiggle free from my fingers and slip back into the water, to swim downstream and see the places I never would.

For sixteen springs I'd watched the river run high and cold with snowmelt, even as the days grew warmer and the light stretched longer into the evenings. One day early in my sixteenth spring, after I'd spent hours getting the garden planted, I was sweaty and sticky and filthy up to my elbows. And I decided, even if the river was still rushing by swift and chill, that it was time for the first bath of the year.

My father was busy bargaining with a customer. I called out to tell him where I was going, left the fish for dinner simmering over the fire, and ran downstream to my favorite pool. The water still had all the bite of the northern ice and snow that it had been not long ago. I splashed and shivered and scraped garden dirt from under my nails until I'd washed a winter's worth of grime off my skin.

I climbed out and dressed myself, settling down on a flat rock to let the sun warm me. Picking up my knife, I cut off one of the young reeds growing in the water and began to make myself a pipe, the way my father had taught me. The reed was only long enough for three holes, but I cut them well and played softly to myself, watching the water beetles skate over the surface of the pond.

"I've heard of the beautiful water maidens who seduce men with their music alone, but I never knew they came so far inland. Tell me, lovely lady, did you tire of the open sea?"

At the first words, I'd rolled into the shallows to put the rock between myself and the intruder. My pipe went flying. Now I raised my head cautiously, reaching for my knife, to look at the man who had startled me.

He had dark hair and eyes so narrow I couldn't see their color; he carried a leather case on his back. His beard needed trimming. And he was laughing at me, at my alarm—but not cruelly. As if he were delighted with his own joke and wanted to share his amusement with me.

"Who are you?" Cold and surprise made my voice high and breathless. "What are you doing here?"

He bowed and spread out empty hands, unthreatening. "Until I heard your music, Enchantress of the Lake, I was merely looking for a ferryman. I was told one lives nearby."

The twist of his smile, one corner higher than the other, almost made me smile myself. He seemed harmless enough. And I could not stay in the water forever. "Wait there," I told him. Watching him carefully, I waded across the pool. A good thing the water wasn't deep, but my plain brown dress was still wet to the knees.

He bowed again to greet me. "Lady of the Lake, you honor me. How may the humble bard Myrddin serve you?" I almost thought he mocked me with his courtesy, as if I were a great lady and not a barefoot ferryman's daughter. But his face was full of friendly mischief. When he named himself a bard, I recognized the shape of the case on his back. Three-cornered, for a harp.

"Duach the ferryman is my father. I'll show you the way to the ford." I tucked my knife into my belt and turned toward the path. He followed at my heels.

"And have you a name as well, Lady of the Lake? Or were you born of mists and water, nameless as the rain?"

"I told you my father. And I am Nimue."

"A name fit for such a lovely spirit of the waters."

"You'll never starve with such a bard's tongue." I glanced at him sideways as we walked, studying his lean face and sharp, jutting nose. I could see now that his eyes were dark blue, like the sky as late sunlight breaks though storm clouds. He had a harpist's restless, long-fingered hands.

My father was back from the river by the time we reached the house. "A bard?" He grinned broadly and bowed his head in respect. "Would you honor our house tonight? It would be nearly dark by the time you crossed the river, and we haven't heard a harp for months, my daughter and I."

"You do me too much honor," Myrddin said gravely. "But I would be glad to stay." He was looking at me.

Before the fire that night, I watched his quick fingers on the harp strings. When my father asked for news, Myrddin spoke of a new warlord, who had been pendragon to one of the southern kings, leader of his army. But now his lord was dead and the former pendragon had kept his power and ruled the kingdom himself. Uther was his name, and half out of fear and half out of respect his men had shortened his title and called him the Dragon.

"I've never heard of him losing a battle he'd set his mind on winning," Myrddin said admiringly. Firelight played off the planes of his lean face. "He has a mind like a Roman's for strategy, and they say he's a demon in a fight. He's even stopped the quarreling among some of the lesser lords and allied them together."

My father laughed. "For how long? Until one sees a chance to stab another in the back? That won't last half a year."

"Maybe not." Myrddin was frowning. "But then, maybe he's the leader to make us strong at last. There could be changes coming to this island."

Duach shrugged. "I doubt I'll live to see them," he said.

I expected Myrddin to be gone early the next morning. But when I woke I found him standing with my father by the wide raft Duach used to ferry customers across the river. The raft needed patching; some of the old logs were split and water-rotten. Myrddin offered to stay a few days, to help my father cut and shape new logs and fit them into place.

That task took them a week. The morning after they finished, Myrddin remarked that he needed a new staff and took the whole day to cut a sapling and shape it to his liking. Then it was that his boots were worn through, and he walked to the village to trade for some leather and begged my help in stitching the new soles on. By the end of two weeks Duach stopped asking him if he would be moving on the next morning, and I stopped worrying that each night would be his last.

Myrddin came with me one day to fish, early in the morning. The sun burned the last of the mist off the water and warmed us as we sat together on a flat, sloping rock near the river's edge.

"Come, little fish," Myrddin crooned as he leaned over to peer into the water. "Come, be our supper tonight . . ." He looked sideways at me to see if I was laughing yet.

"If you talk so loud, you'll scare the fish away," I warned, smiling. But I already knew Myrddin wasn't one to sit quietly without a word.

"Can the fish understand me?" Myrddin looked astonished. "Such intelligent fish you have in this corner of the island, my Lady of the Lake!"

"Fool!" I said, giggling. "And if you had a fish on your line, you'd never know it . . ." *Looking at me that way,* I'd almost said. I glanced away to hide my blush.

"But are you sure these are British fish, my lady?" Myrddin's light tone eased my embarrassment. "Perhaps they're Saxons and can't understand a word we say."

"Perhaps they are," I agreed. "How would we know?"

"Well, if they were Saxon fish, they'd have yellow hair," Myrddin said soberly. I laughed so hard my line jerked in my hands. No self-respecting fish would bite at it. "And they'd have round shields and long swords"—He glanced at me slyly—"and fangs, and horns, and cloven hooves."

"Stop," I protested. "But have you ever seen one, Myrddin?"

"A Saxon? Oh, yes." Myrddin pulled in his hook, now naked of bait, and looked at it mournfully. "I don't think the fish in this river ever bite. You'll have to charm them into our basket, Lady. I've seen plenty of Saxons."

"Are they monsters, like people say?" Saxons burned villages to the ground, cut the ears off their slaves, fed their enemies' bodies to the dogs, and left women pregnant with their devil-children—everyone knew it.

"Bad enough." Myrddin threw his new-baited hook back into the water. "They're warriors like any others, but it's their numbers. One kingdom alone can't hold them off. We need a king to unite us. Like it was in Roman days, one ruler over all the land."

It didn't seem possible to me. Each warlord on the island—and there must have been dozens—guarded his own territory as jealously as a wolf in winter. What could make them bow to one ruler? The Romans had commanded vast armies, and some even said they'd enslaved giants or demons—how else to explain their miles of roads and their great stone cities? How could an ordinary king do anything like that?

Still, Myrddin was a bard, and surely must know more about kings than I did. "A king like that pendragon, Uther?" I asked, remembering what Myrddin had said on his first night with us.

"He may be the one." Myrddin was looking out across the river. "Think, Nimue, what it would be like. Think what we could do if we didn't spend all our time fighting Saxons, and Picts, and Irish, and each other . . ."

I wondered what this king of his, this great ruler, would do if there were no more wars. Wasn't that what a king did, ride into battle? What would his warband do if they couldn't fight? Sit by the fire all day like old women? But I didn't say this to Myrddin. I liked the way his dark blue eyes looked dreamily out across the water.

We didn't catch anything that day, or most of the days we sat beside the river. There were some days we didn't fish at all, but just wandered along the bank. I showed Myrddin the most beautiful places I'd found in my sixteen years by the river—smooth pools fringed with lacy ferns, white waterfalls, islands where herons nested. In the evenings Myrddin would play his harp and sing, or tell the old tales, and the people of the village crowded our little house to hear him.

As he sang of kings and warriors, battles and love, I marveled, thinking that he had actually *seen* kings and warlords and the distant kingdoms he told tales about. And yet with everything he'd seen, he still seemed content to stay here, in this nameless village. Almost as if there was something here he thought was valuable.

There came an evening Myrddin let his harp sit silent for once and went out to study the stars. My father and I sat together in the warm, dark circle of our house. I was mending; Duach was carving fishhooks. Faint light drifted in from the smoke hole above the dying fire. "Has he asked you yet?" my father said, not looking up from the tiny splinters of wood on his lap.

"Who? Asked me what?" Half my mind was on my mending, the other half listening to the whispering of the river, soft as breath.

"Myrddin, of course. Asked you to marry him."

My hands dropped to my lap. "Do you think he will?"

"Why else has he been staying here these weeks? Nimue?" He looked up at last. "Think of it now. So when he asks, you will know what to say."

After several minutes of silence, I moved to sit on the floor beside his stool. "You would be lonely without me."

His hand touched my hair. "Lonely, yes. But I'm not such a fool . . ." He put two fingers under my chin, tipping my head back so that I had to look at him. "Child, I never thought you would stay here forever. If I will be lonely, it would be nothing to what you would feel when I am gone. You are sixteen, Nimue. It is time you were married, time you had children."

I had heard those words before, from the village women who had shared my mothering among them after my own mother died giving life to me. They'd warned me what happens to girls who wait too long: no husband, no babies; ending as a lonely, bitter crone. But I knew if I married one of the village boys, I'd lose any chance I might ever have had to find out where the river went, to see for myself the places in the travelers' tales.

Now if I married Myrddin . . .

"If he asks," I told Duach, "I will say yes."

But Myrddin didn't ask, and as slow days went by I decided that he never would. He was a bard, after all, a keeper of the old law, a man who could stand before kings. What would he want with a ferryman's daughter? Still, I loved his smile when he made me laugh, loved hearing his stories, listening to him play the harp. Maybe, if all he left me with was his child when he went off into the wide world—maybe that would be enough.

Some days after my talk with Duach I took Myrddin to one of my favorite places, a small clearing in the forest with a great oak tree in its center. The trunk was hollow, and I was still thin enough to slip inside. Myrddin leaned his head back to look up at the branches high above us.

"As old as this island, it is." He laid his hand reverently on the rough bark. "In the old days it would have been a holy tree. And mistletoe!" He pulled a sprig of the plant free and tucked it into my hair. "Mistletoe for a bride. For strong sons and daughters." I ducked my head because I was sure my smile looked foolish. Myrddin put his hand on my shoulder. "Nimue . . ."

I felt as if every inch of my skin was listening for his next word.

"*The sword . . .*"

Myrddin's voice was a bare whisper, harsh as dry leaves rattling in the wind. Shocked, I looked up to see all the life gone from his face, as suddenly as if two fingers had pinched a candlewick and smothered the flame between them. Only his eyes moved; cold and distant, they watched things I could not see.

"Myrddin," I whispered. "Myrddin!" He didn't hear.

"Didn't I tell you, my lord? The day is yours." His head turned a little; he seemed to be speaking to someone standing next to me. I shrank from the weight of his hand on my shoulder, from the ghost he almost made me see beside me. *"They remember that sword,"* he whispered, and smiled in triumph. *"Your father's sword. . ."*

Then the man I knew came back behind the eyes. "Nimue!" He grasped both my arms, his face alight. I tried to pull away, but he didn't seem to notice. "It will happen, Nimue! Even his son will rule. It will happen! It will!" he repeated, shaking me, his fingers driving bruises into my arms.

I managed a faint sound as I wrenched myself from his grasp and stumbled back. Myrddin's grin vanished. "Nimue, sweet, did I frighten you?" he whispered.

"Don't touch me!" I backed away from his outstretched hand.

"You don't have to be afraid." His words came slowly. "I won't hurt you, Nimue. I would never—you don't have to be afraid of me. Please." His hand trembled.

"What are you?" I couldn't raise my voice above a whisper.

"My mother always called me a devil's son." He let his hand fall. "They drove me out of the village one year when the harvest was bad. I was eight years old." He turned away from me. "They were afraid of me too."

My fear was still there, a cold taste in the back of my throat. But it had been swallowed up in a wave of pity, like a rock vanishing under the spring flood. I remembered Myrddin laughing with me by the river. I saw a helpless boy driven out into the forest, saw the man I wanted for my husband looking across the clearing, at anything but me.

"I'll go," Myrddin said angrily. "You don't have to worry. I'll leave today, I never should have stayed."

"No," I said softly. I wouldn't be like the others. I wouldn't fear him. I would love him, whatever he was, whatever unearthly visions he saw. And maybe then he would love me enough to take me with him.

"Don't go," I said. Myrddin didn't turn or look at me, so I went to put my arms around him. "I'm not afraid of you," I whispered. A promise. A bargain.

Myrddin stood for a moment without moving, and then he wrapped his arms around me, holding me so tightly I could hardly breathe.

2

WE WERE MARRIED IN THE OLD WAY, since there was no priest in our village. A sheep was slaughtered for the feast, and the cooking had gone on for three days beforehand. There was mistletoe twined in the band of flowers around my hair. Duach joined our hands before the village, and Myrddin gave three gold rings from his fingers as my bride price. They were too large for my hands, so I wore them on a leather thong around my neck. While the feast continued outside, Myrddin and I went into the house and pulled the deerskin close over the door. We were married to the sounds of laughter and talk and out-of-tune singing.

Early the next morning Duach ferried us across the river. He held me close for a long time and I cried a little. Suddenly the world I'd longed to see seemed much too wide, and I almost gave Myrddin back his rings and begged Duach to take me home. But at last I dried my tears and set out on the road with my new husband.

We'd walk all day and sleep on the grass by the roadside, or stay the night in a farmhouse or shepherd's cottage. Most people were glad to see us, but some frowned with suspicion. "We've had no travelers here for three, four years now," one woman said shortly, standing with her arms crossed in the doorway of her home to bar us out. "Thieves or spies, more likely. Can't you see there's nothing left to steal?"

Myrddin took my arm as I drew an indignant breath. "We're no threat to you," he said quietly. "We'll go on."

By the old law a bard is welcome for three nights at any house he comes to, king's court or beggar's hut. But when I demanded why Myrddin hadn't shown her his harp, he only shook his head. "They don't keep the old law here," he said as we walked on. "Or Roman law, or any law except fear everyone, trust no one. And why should they? Times are hard enough for them. That's why we need—"

Out of the corner of his eye he saw me roll my eyes at the heavens for patience. I'd heard his talk of why we needed a strong leader like Uther the Dragon a good many times already. I'd even caught some of his enthusiasm and was growing eager to see this new king who was going to save us all. But for now my feet hurt and I was hungry.

"All right, I talk too much." Myrddin caught my hand and squeezed it. "There's a village not far from here; we can be there by nightfall if we hurry. I've stayed there before."

The sunlight was darkening to deep gold when Myrddin, slowing his pace, said we must be near the village he remembered. But he was frowning, and I realized that I could hear nothing—no children shouting, no dogs barking at the scent of strangers, no cows bellowing to be milked. A breeze drifted by us, but I could smell no wood smoke, nothing like barley bread baking or stew full of mutton and turnips simmering over the coals.

Myrddin, ahead of me, had stopped short as he turned a bend in the path. I moved close to him and looked over his shoulder.

There were five or six houses grouped together in a circle. Farmers, Myrddin told me later, a couple of shepherds, a potter who made bowls and jugs from clay he dug from the nearby riverbank. What was left of the wooden walls of the houses was black and charred, the thatched roofs burnt to ash. There were bodies lying like lumps of wet rags in the grass, and a heavy smell like rotten fish made my stomach heave and my throat close up. No one had been left to bury them.

I remembered, strangely, the time a sparrow had blundered down the smoke hole of my father's house and, in a panic, battered itself to death against the walls. I put my hands against my mouth to smother the sound rising in my throat. I sounded like that bird.

Myrddin turned abruptly. "Let's go. There's nothing—" Pulling me back, he almost stumbled over something lying near the path at his feet.

Dreading it, I looked down. The body of a dog lay curled in a small hollow in the grass, the ground around it black with old blood. I stared fixedly at it. A villageful of dead people behind me and I stared down at the body of a dog, its fur the soft gold of ripe grain, its paws—

Its paws had been hacked off at the first joint. There was no other wound that I could see. Someone had cut its feet off while it was alive and left it to crawl away and bleed to death slowly, alone.

Myrddin pulled me roughly after him, walking quickly back to the main road. I pressed my hand hard against my mouth and swallowed until I could speak.

"Who—?" I panted at Myrddin's back. "Who would do that—?"

"Saxon raiders," Myrddin said grimly. He slowed down a little so that I could keep up with him. "Or Irish slavers, or Picts from the north, or some king's warband with nothing better to do—" He shrugged, but his face was chalky pale. "Anyone. Anyone could have done that. Nimue, I've seen it over and over. I can't count the villages I've come back to and found nothing but bones. It isn't safe anywhere. Not anymore."

We didn't light a fire that night, and slept well back from the roadside, wrapped in our cloaks. In truth I didn't sleep much at all. We'd always been safe in our village, too far inland to be reached by Irish slavers, too far west to be in danger from Saxon warbands. Besides, my father always said, it's bad luck to kill a ferryman; you never know when you might want to get back across the river again.

But I'd seen enough travelers, fleeing their ruined villages with only the clothes on their backs. Their tales of fire and robbery and slaughter hadn't been ones I'd loved to listen to. Duach usually let them cross the river for free, on their way to kin, or a lord who might protect them, or just *away* from the wreck of their lives. I huddled into Myrddin's arms, my back against his chest, but I couldn't keep my eyes closed.

I thought Myrddin was asleep. Then he spoke, his breath whispering into my hair. "It happened to my village. I went back after I became a bard. I wanted to show them . . ." His voice trailed off. "But there was nothing there. You couldn't see where the houses had been. No one nearby even remembered what had happened."

I took one of his hands and rubbed it against my cheek, tears welling up in my eyes. Myrddin wrapped me tighter in his arms. "You see?" he murmured. "You see why we need this king? To keep law here, everywhere . . ." I lay staring into the darkness as if my watchfulness could keep us safe when it wasn't safe anywhere. Not anymore.

BUT IF THERE WAS ANYTHING that could have kept us safe, it would have been the wall of Caerleon. At least I thought so the first time I saw Uther the Dragon's city. Myrddin had told me that it was a Roman fortress, where the legions had stayed before they'd all marched away and left their stone towns and walls and roads to crumble and fall. But neither his words nor my daydreams had prepared me for the sight of a stone wall taller than my head, circling a town that held more men and women and children, horses and sheep and pigs and cattle and chickens, than I'd known there were in the world.

Myrddin wasn't at all disturbed by what seemed to me a vast crowd as we entered by the gates, the great wooden doors wide open to let the townsfolk in and out. He walked easily among the people, who in their turn hurried by without giving us a second glance. A woman in a fine red cloak walked past with a basket full of bread on her hip. Another emptied a pot of bones and rotten vegetables into the gutter, adding to a pile of garbage already waist high and smothered in buzzing black flies.

We stopped to let a shepherd hustle his flock through the street, sheep jostling about our knees, and I stared around me at the buildings on either side—some stone, some wood, roofed with slate or thatch, some full of people and others empty, with unshuttered windows gaping open, roofs sagging, walls leaning. But strangest of all, they were square, with four corners, in the Roman style. I'd never seen a house that wasn't a circle, and I gaped at these, wondering how people ever felt at home inside of them.

Myrddin headed for the town center as if he knew exactly where everything was, and stopped to ask a man by the well where the lord might be found. Frowning, the man looked us over, spat thoughtfully into the water, and said at last, "The Dragon. He's gone to see to repairs on the wall. But if you're thinking of staying here, you'll call him king, same as the rest of us." He gave us a final disdainful glance and waved us in the right direction.

With my eye out for a tall and handsome hero-king out of the old stories, I overlooked Uther entirely. Shorter than most of the men at his side, his brown hair and beard streaked with iron gray, I only knew him for the king when he stepped forward to meet Myrddin.

"A bard?" His gaze swept Myrddin from head to foot and returned to watching the men who were working on the wall, struggling to heave mismatched stones into a gap wide enough for two to walk through shoulder to shoulder. "Well, we have not heard music for a while," Uther said indifferently. "You may play for the court tonight, and have lodging here."

In the old days, a king would have begged a bard to honor his court. I grew warm with anger on Myrddin's behalf, but my husband only bowed and thanked Uther humbly.

The king tossed one glance in my direction. His looks were as effective as another man's commands; Myrddin drew me forward. "I beg leave to present my wife. The lady Nimue."

I managed an awkward curtsy, miserably aware of my dirty skirt and bedraggled hair. I felt sure Uther would have given Myrddin more respect if he had not been wived with a dusty peasant girl. The king nodded once to me, and dismissed us both by turning his back.

Myrddin was jubilant. As soon as we were out of Uther's hearing he burst into speech. "Now *that* is a king, Nimue! Did you see?" He swung around to face me, grabbing hold of both my hands. "'Call him king,' the man said. *Lord* is not enough of a title for him. Someday it will be *emperor,* just like a Roman!"

"Myrddin!" Impatiently, I freed my hands from his. "He dismissed you like a servant! He did not even thank you for honoring his court!"

Myrddin laughed. "What does a man like that need with courtesy? He is a warrior, not a bard." His smile was sly. "But my harp will win me a place at his court, and from there, I hope, my counsel will win me his respect and his ear." He leaned forward to kiss me happily. "Come, my Lady of the Lake. Let's find our lodgings. If I'm going to play before a king tonight, I need to shave first."

Uther gave Myrddin and me a place of honor at the high table, but he didn't speak to us, or look up when Myrddin rose to sing. I was tired from all the walking we'd done that day, and smoke from the candles and the hearth fire stung my eyes; they kept drifting shut. Dreamily, I heard scraps of different conversations, from Uther and some of his counselors on my right, from a few young warriors to my left. One of them looked barely old enough to wear a sword, and he sounded as if he'd drunk a little too freely.

"Why should I be quiet? Everyone knows—"

"He promised us the stone as tribute, and he's already late. Tell him I don't care—" I could already recognize the king's voice: flat, untouched by emotion.

"Ambrosius was our lord—" The young warrior again, and perhaps louder than he knew.

"Shut your mouth, you're—"

"I want that wall finished before the planting's done."

"I'm not afraid to say it! No one knows how he died, and everyone's scared to open their mouths!"

It was the young man's bad luck that his last sentence fell during a pause in Myrddin's song. Myrddin hurried the next verse to cover the heavy silence that settled over the high table. I opened my eyes to see the young warrior with the brash tongue sit upright, looking sick, and suddenly push his bench back and bolt from the hall with a hand over his mouth. One of his friends stood up to follow him, then caught Uther's eye and quickly sat down again.

Myrddin returned to sit beside me, swallowing half a cup of ale to ease his throat. He was whispering, "How was the song?" when we heard a commotion at the other end of the hall. People were getting up from their benches, crowding around the door. Voices were raised, but I couldn't distinguish words.

"What is it?" I twisted, trying to get a glimpse.

Myrddin shrugged. "I'll go see." He was back in a few minutes, slipping into his seat. "An accident," he said. "One of the soldiers slipped in the courtyard, cracked his skull wide open on the stones. Blind drunk, he was. The one that was sitting right there."

His eyes, fixed on mine, stopped my words in my throat. "I'd better sing again," he murmured, reaching for his harp. "Did it sound all right last time?" He was gone before I could answer.

IT DIDN'T TAKE LONG FOR UTHER to discover that his new bard had talents beyond flattery and pretty tunes. The warlord had no use for music, but he soon came to value a counselor with a mind full of history and politics, an unquestioning loyalty to his kingship, and an uncanny knowledge of things to come. Myrddin abandoned his harp almost entirely, only playing for my ears when we were alone late at night.

Myrddin never wavered in his conviction that Uther was the great leader he had foreseen. But the king made me uneasy. I avoided him much as possible—easily done, since he ignored me completely—and did my best, as the months went by, to forget what had happened to the young warrior our first night at the court. Since no one ever spoke of it, I could almost believe that I had dreamed it, or simply manage not to think of it at all.

For months I saw my husband mostly at night, for his days were spent at Uther's side. Before my marriage I had often enough passed days alone, wandering up and down the riverbanks.

But I had never felt lonely then as I did waiting in that strange square room for Myrddin to return.

I would sit and sew with the ladies of the court when I could, although that was little better. I doubt they truly meant to be unkind, but they had all, it seemed to me, known one another for years, and those that weren't sisters were cousins, or kin by marriage or fosterage. Often they would all burst into laughter at a single word, while I stared dumbly down at my needle and waited for the joke to be explained to me.

I made new dresses for myself, from linen finer than any I had ever worn before. I wove a new cloak for Myrddin of dark gray wool, and worked an intricate border of red and green around the hem. That cloak kept my hands and eyes busy for a good two months. And when I had nothing else to do I spun thread, miles of it, wondering if I'd exchanged the sight of my river flowing by for nothing more exciting than watching an endless skein of thread stretch straight and fine between my fingers.

I was spinning the day I first met the lady Igrayne. Humming one of Myrddin's songs to myself, I sat in a corner of the hall away from the other women, looking out a window into a quiet stone courtyard. I didn't need to look down at my hands to know that the thread was coming well; I could feel the soft tufts of wool knitting themselves together into a smooth, even cord between my fingers, pulled thin by the weight of the spindle stone spinning near my feet.

Someone coughed a little, very quietly. I looked up in surprise to see a pale, dark-haired woman standing next to me.

"Isn't your name Nimue? I am Igrayne." My surprise at being addressed only made her smile wider. She had arrived at the court a week or so ago, with the first warm days of summer. Her husband was a young southern lord, Cawdor, considering an alliance with Uther. Everyone seemed to admire her, and I'd heard the women whispering that her family was of the blood of the ancient kings, before the Romans came. I couldn't imagine why she wanted to speak with me.

She sat down gracefully on the bench beside me. "Isn't your

husband the bard who is always with Uther? You must beg him to play for us tonight. I love music, and we have not heard a harp at our court for months." She touched my thread, swinging forgotten between my fingers. "What good hands you have for this; I never have the patience for it." I could tell it was a lie, looking at the fine sewing she spread across her lap, but it was so kindly meant that I smiled back.

Myrddin brought out his long-unused harp that night and said that he would sing of the war fought over Branwen, daughter of Llyr, the loveliest maiden in the island, for surely her spirit had been born on earth again and was with us that night. Even Uther, for once, did not talk during the song, but sat silent, with his brooding gaze locked on Igrayne's face.

It was not only Uther who was fascinated by Igrayne. Everyone loved her—her beauty, her grace, her quick laughter. Her smile was the warmest thing in that stony Roman city, and I never saw it brighter than when she spoke about her children. "Two girls, Elen and Morgan," she told me one day as we sat sewing in the hall as usual. "Morgan has only just turned four, and Elen's six. And she takes such care of her sister! They have a nurse, but really, it's Elen who looks after Morgan. She's into everything, that one. Once we had to pull her out of the cow pond!" She sighed and looked wistful. "They'll have grown so much by the time we're home again." Suddenly she stabbed her needle into the dress she was sewing and tossed it to one side. "It's much too fine a day to spend it trapped indoors. Enough!" She leaned down to snatch my spindle out of the air and wind the thread around it. "You must have enough thread by now to clothe everyone in Caerleon. Come out and walk with me."

We wandered along by the city wall, picking our way over pieces of fallen stone. The bright sun made Igrayne's hair shine with glossy light. "These alliance talks take so long!" Igrayne complained. "Cawdor knows he's going to agree to whatever Uther asks. Why he has to drag his feet so . . ." She laughed. "It can hardly be for the sake of Uther's company!"

I laughed too; it was so seldom anyone at the court said anything frank about Uther. Indeed, they rarely spoke of him at all, as if the mention of his name would conjure him, demonlike, from the shadows.

"Are you sure," I asked a little shyly, "about the alliance? Uther is—" *Not to be trusted,* I wanted to say. *Haven't you noticed the way he looks at you?* But there were people coming up behind us. I shut my mouth on the words.

Igrayne shrugged. She sat down on a table-sized piece of fallen stone and patted the spot next to her, inviting me to join her. "Well, we need the alliance, my dear, and that's the truth." Her face, usually so quick to change expression, was sad and still. "Our land is on the coast, and the sea raiders come from Ireland. We lose too much of the harvest every year. And they take people for slaves." She sighed. "Uther isn't charming, I grant you, but if we were allied with him, we could defend our land."

And after all, what could Uther do? He might look at Igrayne with that disquieting stare, but even Uther wouldn't harm a guest. And Igrayne surely knew much more than I did about such things. So I smiled back at her and let my warning stay unspoken.

"And you?" Igrayne put her hand on mine and squeezed. "When are you planning to have some children with that handsome bard of yours?"

I laughed and put a hand over my stomach. "Soon, I hope!" For months I had been looking enviously at other women with their swollen bellies. Perhaps a baby would wrest some of Myrddin's attention away from Uther and give it back to me.

"I have some herbs I can give you. I don't take them when I'm traveling, but when we're back home . . ." Igrayne winked mischievously. "I love the girls dearly, but we need a son."

"I'm sure you'll have one."

"And we'll bring him here to play with yours!" We laughed together. "Or no, Nimue, I have a better idea. You have a girl, and when they're old enough we'll marry them off. Isn't that an excellent plan?"

I think perhaps the gods don't approve when mortals are too pleased with their own plans.

3

NE NIGHT A FEW DAYS LATER, as I was returning to our chamber, I heard Igrayne's voice, low and urgent, calling me. I turned as she came hurrying up. In the dark of night, her eyes were pools of shadow in her pale face. It was only when she came closer that I saw the trickle of blood from her nose and her cut, swelling lip.

I caught at her hands. "What happened?" I could imagine robbery, murder, every kind of terror.

"Uther—" She gripped my hands hard and took a deep breath to steady herself. "We are leaving, Nimue. I had to tell you—"

"Uther? What did he do?"

Freeing one hand from mine, she touched her mouth and pulled her cloak back to show me her dress, ripped at the shoulder seam halfway down the arm. "We will not stay another hour, Nimue. He tried to—"

"Are you hurt? Did he—" My selfish grief at the idea of losing my only friend was lost in my fear for her.

Her bloody lip curled back from her teeth. For the first time I saw a hardness in her, and remembered that she was of the blood of the old kings. "He would never have touched another woman if he had! We are leaving—tonight. Cawdor wanted to kill Uther, but we are alone here. When a host has no honor, the guests are prey. But I wouldn't leave without saying good-bye to you."

"Go quickly," I urged, though I didn't let go of her hands.

"Nimue, won't you come with us? Our court is not as grand as this, but we can support a bard. You and Myrddin could come tonight. Why not?"

I thought that would be perfect happiness, to live with my friend and my husband somewhere safe, far to the south, away from Uther. But I knew Myrddin would never agree to leave his king. I shook my head and kissed Igrayne good-bye. Before the hour was over, she and her husband were gone, so secretly that hardly anyone knew. Half of their servants were left behind, to stay or make their way home as best they might.

I waited among the bed furs for a long time that night, intending to demand of Myrddin how he could serve a king who would rape another man's wife, kill one of his own warriors, maybe even murder his lord. But Myrddin stayed away so long I fell asleep in spite of my intentions, and did not stir even when he returned and slipped into the bed beside me. Sometime in the night his voice woke me, only a whisper, but deep and loud enough to shake me out of sleep.

"She is weeping." There was such sorrow in his voice that my throat went tight. Raising myself on one elbow, I saw that his eyes were open, staring blankly out into the night; his cheeks were silver with tears and moonlight.

He did not speak to me of this vision in the morning. But we hardly had time to speak of anything. We had only been awake a few minutes when Uther discovered that Igrayne and her husband were gone.

Uther's rage was all the more terrifying for being completely silent. He went riding after them with a score of his own men, and more to follow when they were armed and mounted. Myrddin went with him.

Branwen, Llyr's daughter, indeed.

IT WAS WEARY MONTHS BEFORE they came back, and their horses walked through snow. I ran with the rest of the court to see them returning. Uther was full of cold self-satisfaction, Myrddin, wrapped in the cloak I had made for him, quiet and unhappy beside him. And Igrayne—

She rode a white mare, and the fur on her hood made a soft, snow-white frame for her pale face. Her mouth was frozen, her dark eyes wide and empty. When I ran to help her down, her hands were icy cold and she didn't speak a word.

Cursing Uther under my breath, I led Igrayne to my chamber. I wrapped her in furs and tried to warm her frozen hands, held hot wine to her lips, but she wouldn't drink. Her eyes never strayed to my face. I thought she didn't know me, or even where she was. But then she spoke.

"He killed him, Nimue." Her voice was simple and sweet, steeped in a sorrow so great it seemed untouched by emotion. "He killed him unarmed, in our marriage bed. And he had me in his blood." She swayed as if a wind had touched her. I made meaningless sounds, aching to comfort her, but she said nothing more, and lay down in the furs and slept like a child. Bending over her, I saw tears slipping from under her closed eyelids, but her face held a pale, deathlike peace.

I thought I heard a sound, or maybe Myrddin's presence was enough to make me turn. He stood in the doorway, looking at Igrayne, and I have no words for the look on his face. I started to go to him, but he turned suddenly and left, and I was afraid to leave Igrayne alone to follow him.

There was a great feast that night, to celebrate Uther's safe return and his marriage. Igrayne sat statue-cold and still beside the king. I listened in silence while Myrddin sang of glory and valor. My fury burst forth when Myrddin and I were alone in our chamber for the night.

"How can you *serve* this man?" I shrieked, not caring for once who heard me. "Have you seen her? Do you know what he did? He killed her just as if he had cut her throat!" Myrddin stood mute before me, watching me miserably. "Do you know what he did?" I demanded again. "Have you seen?"

"Know? I was there!" His voice splintered. "I watched him kill Cawdor. I stood outside the door!" He choked and then continued, pleading. "Nimue, don't you understand? It must be—"

"Understand?" I breathed, drawing back from him. "You are as bad as he is, I understand! You *knew*? You let him do that, and you still serve him?"

"I must!" He came closer, his face intent. "Nimue, listen—it is their son. Their child is the one who must rule! I thought it was Uther, but I was wrong. Their son will be the great king! I have seen—"

I took a step back. "You are mad!"

"And *you* are like the rest of them. Afraid of me!" He was angry, but suddenly he was blinking back tears. Before I could move, he dropped to his knees and wrapped his arms around my waist. "Please, please, don't be afraid," he begged. "My love, my heart, if you fear me too, I *will* go mad. You said you were not afraid . . ."

"I wasn't," I whispered. I didn't say, *I am now*. When the spring flood goes down, the rock is still there.

But I didn't move away. I'd promised him. I'd given my word.

Later that night, beside me under the furs, he spoke feverishly of Uther and Igrayne's son. A king crowned with justice, uniting the scattered kingdoms, ruling in peace and strength. "And he is conceived already, Nimue! I saw it that night I stood outside the door. She bears the greatest king this land will ever know."

I thought of Igrayne in her bloody marriage bed and wept, silent in the dark, as Myrddin talked on.

IT SEEMED THAT IGRAYNE'S GRIEF had devoured her. She hardly spoke, never smiled, and walked through her days like a ghost. There were times I wondered if she were planning to join her dead lord.

I think I might have hated Myrddin if he hadn't been nearly as miserable himself. "Her children are safe," he said, the morning after their return. He kept his eyes fixed on the boot he was lacing up. "The nurse took them, to the north, I think. I tried to tell Igrayne when we were on the road, but I don't think she heard me. You tell her."

I did, and I was grateful to him, for it was the only thing that brought Igrayne any comfort at all. But it seemed as if she didn't dare trust the news, for nearly every day she would ask again, "But my children, Nimue? They're safe? You said they're safe?" And I would tell her, again and again, that her daughters were well, that they would grow up happy, safe in the north country, far away from Uther.

I spent as much time as I could with Igrayne, braiding her hair, coaxing her to eat, holding her while she cried. But whenever I was with her, a small stone of dread lodged itself in my throat, and I couldn't swallow it away. What if it had been me, my fear whispered. What if I had been the one who stood between Myrddin and his king? Which of us would he have chosen?

Since I couldn't answer the question I did my best to stop asking it. But it never quite left my mind.

Myrddin had seen truly; Igrayne was pregnant. It might, of course, have happened on any night during their two-week journey back from Cornwall. But Myrddin was certain, and I saw no reason to doubt him, that this new life had begun the night Uther had taken the castle and killed Igrayne's unarmed lord.

In a few months I knew something Myrddin had not foreseen. I had conceived as well.

Whenever I put both hands over my belly and felt the small, astonishing life growing there, I thought that this was something all our own—a child, Myrddin's and mine. And maybe if I tried hard enough, this was something I could keep safe from politics and prophecies and dark visions of the future.

Igrayne suffered through her long labor with hardly a sound, though her wasted hands left black bruises on mine. Her little son was small and wrinkled, with dark eyes and tufts of thistledown hair that made him look absurdly ancient. I thought it would give Igrayne joy to see him, but after one weary look she pushed him aside and closed her eyes. So I held the baby and soothed him to sleep.

Arthur, they named him. Arthur ap Uther, the Dragon's son.

When my own time came early, a few days later, I couldn't understand how Igrayne had endured her labor so silently. I thought the world was being ripped apart, and Olwen the midwife said in exasperation that I shrieked louder than a birthing cow. "And so would you!" I gasped indignantly, and she laughed and said, "And so I did. Push now, push!" When she put my tiny son in my arms at last, I started to shake, and Myrddin, who came to kneel beside us, put his arm tight around me. Resentful of the light, the baby burrowed his face into my breasts, his tiny eyes shut tight. Myrddin touched his round red cheek gingerly with one finger.

I hoped his eyes would stay blue, like Myrddin's, but they darkened to deep brown after a few weeks. We named him Duach, for my father.

Igrayne's milk failed after a few days, and since I was fuller than a cow with two calves, I suckled both children. Uther was coldly pleased to have a son, but he took no real interest in the boy. Igrayne hardly seemed to notice Arthur at all. So I cared for them both, and soon almost felt as if I had borne twins. Both boys slept between Myrddin and me at night, since Uther refused to have his sleep disturbed by the crying of his son.

A few months after their birth I sat with both children at the high table one night. I tickled Arthur's nose with the end of my braid. The meal was over, but Uther was still speaking with his counselors. As always, Igrayne sat stone-still and silent by his side, her untouched plate before her. I wondered why he had gone to so much trouble to win her, when he hardly noticed her now.

"What do you say, my hawk?" Uther asked, turning to face Myrddin. "Will I win it?" *Hawk* was his name for his tame prophet. Farsighted, he meant, and captive, I thought, as tethered and obedient as any trained bird. "What have you foreseen?"

"I have not seen my lord losing," Myrddin said carefully.

Uther was satisfied. "If I win this, no one will challenge my rule. Right, my hawk?"

"All know my lord is already the greatest king of this land." Uther was turning away, but Myrddin spoke again, in a voice drained of life and warmth, a flat whisper that still reached every ear. *"And the son will be far greater than the father. The father's name will fade beside the son's and none will remember it. The son—"*

Uther's arm swept cups and bowls from the tabletop. His clenched fist halted an inch from Myrddin's face. "Silence, traitor, or I will have your head," he growled.

Myrddin woke enough from his trance to flinch from Uther's hand and stammer apologies, blaming his words on a false dream, a devil's sending. Uther let his gaze withdraw from his bard and fall on me. Trembling, I took a child under each arm and fled from the hall.

I was sleepless under the furs when Myrddin returned. He hesitated in the doorway and then groped his way, as if blind or drunk, to the bed. He dropped to his knees beside me and in the dim moonlight I saw his face, haggard with fear.

"Myrddin, what is it?"

His words seemed to stumble through a great distance. "There is danger, Nimue. There is great danger here, and I cannot see it . . ." His fingers were icy; I thought his hand would crush mine.

"Yes, there is danger! Uther will never forgive what you said to him. We must leave, Myrddin! Now, tonight!"

He shook his head impatiently. "No, not for me, he needs me. It is the boy, Nimue, the little boy . . ."

I sat upright in the furs, clutching at Myrddin's arm. "Duach?" Myrddin shook his head again.

"I saw them together, father and son. Each had a sword . . ."

I wanted to shake him. "Myrddin, speak sense! Is it Arthur?" He nodded, shivering. "Who will die, Myrddin?" I demanded. "Arthur or Uther? Who will die?"

He looked at me, startled, trembling so hard he could barely speak. "No, not Arthur and Uther. It was Arthur and his son." He would say nothing more, and crawled under the furs to sleep like a dead man.

But in the morning he was still awake before me. I was pulled out of sleep by his hand on my shoulder, his voice in my ear. "Nimue, listen. I know what we must do."

"Myrddin?" Sleepily I sat up, reaching out a hand to touch both Arthur and Duach, as if they might have vanished in the night. But they were still there, huddled in the furs between Myrddin and myself. Arthur stirred a little as my fingers brushed his soft, fair hair. Duach's hair had been darker at first, but it was slowly starting to lighten to nearly the shade of Arthur's.

Myrddin was sitting upright in the bed, still in the clothes he had worn last night, with the furs clutched around his shoulders. The darkness in the window behind him was just starting to fade with the early dawn. "Listen, Nimue," he said. He bent forward, his voice urgent. "We must save him."

I blinked at him, still a little stupid with sleep. Yes, there were many people we must save, it seemed to me, and ourselves not the least among them. I was preparing to insist that we flee Uther's court when Myrddin spoke again.

"We must leave. As soon as we can."

I let out a breath I hadn't known I was holding. Myrddin had made his choice at last. He'd chosen his family over his king—me, Duach, us.

"Yes, soon!" I leaned forward to seize one of his hands with both of mine. "We'll be free of him, Myrddin. We'll be safe."

He nodded. "We'll take Arthur."

Something cold and hard seemed to be blocking my throat. It was hard to speak around it. "Myrddin, think. Have sense." I kept my voice calm. He was tired, that was all, shaken by his latest vision. He wasn't thinking clearly. "If we take Arthur, Uther will follow us. You know he will."

"No," Myrddin said. His eyes didn't seem to focus on me at all, but he brought his other hand to hold both of mine trapped between his. "Listen, now, Nimue. We'll tell Uther that you want to take Duach to see your father. He'll be glad enough to see the back of me for a while, he won't object. But it's Arthur we'll take. Uther's hardly looked at the boy; he will notice no difference—"

I wrenched my hands away from his. "Mad!" I shouted.

"You're mad, do you think I'd"— I snatched Duach up and stumbled off the bed, backing away—"leave my own child here?" Duach squirmed in my arms and began to cry.

"Nimue!" Myrddin stood up, facing me across the bed. The furs fell in a heap around his feet. "Do you think that of me? That I'd abandon my own son? Nimue, you can't believe—"

"What then?" I gave Duach my finger to suck and he quieted. But I still held him tight, warily. The door to our chamber was at my back.

"Listen, and I'll tell you." Myrddin didn't move, but he kept his eyes on me. "We can't leave Arthur here, Nimue. His father will do some harm to him. This child is the great king, Nimue! I—we—must protect him."

"By leaving your own son to face danger in his place?" I spat, furious. If he took a step toward me I would run.

"No!" Myrddin nearly shouted his answer. "We will come back for Duach, Nimue. Can you think otherwise? We'll find a home for Arthur, a family to take care of him. When we come back, we'll tell them all that our own son sickened and died on the road. Then we'll take Duach. We'll run."

"Then let's run now." Duach's tiny body was so warm against mine; I thought if I let him go I might be cold for the rest of my life. "We'll take them both and run." I felt an instant's guilt for the betrayal of Igrayne in such a proposal. But she was so lost in her own grief that she paid no more attention to the boy than Uther did.

Myrddin was shaking his head. "Travel with two children? It will be hard enough with just one, and Uther's men on our trail."

"But—Duach!" I clutched him close. "We can't leave him here with Uther!"

"He will be safe," Myrddin insisted. "I've seen no danger for him. Uther won't act at once. We have time, Nimue."

"You can't be sure."

"I am. Trust me." I hesitated. "Nimue. Would you take our son, and go, and leave Arthur here? Leave him with his father?"

My eyes went to Igrayne's son, still sleeping peacefully in the bed furs. There was little enough I could do to help Igrayne in the hell her life had become. But didn't I owe it to her to protect the son she couldn't nurse, couldn't care for, couldn't love?

"Do you swear—" I looked back at Myrddin. "Do you swear to me that Duach would be in no danger?"

Maybe it was only how hard I was listening for his answer that made it seem such a long time in coming. But when he spoke at last, I felt the force of belief in his voice. "I swear it by every god, Nimue!"

I didn't run after all as he came around the bed, close to my side. "Nimue? Will you help me in this?"

My own son, my friend's son—if we could save them both, and save ourselves, and be free of Uther at last . . .

"Yes," I whispered.

4

THER WAS NOT RELUCTANT to grant his bard leave to depart for a few weeks' time. Myrddin's presence was a constant reminder of that ill-timed vision, not only to the king but to the rest of the court as well. In those few days while we hastily prepared for our journey, hardly anyone spoke to us, as if Uther's displeasure were as contagious as the plague.

We easily found a wet nurse for Duach. There were always enough women in the city who'd lost a child in birthing or shortly after. I thought I would ruin Myrddin's entire plan by bursting into tears when I handed the baby to her. But Myrddin's arm around my shoulders both steadied me and reminded me of our danger. If Uther hadn't judged us traitors already, he surely would now, the second I called my own son by the name of his.

So I only smiled and told the nurse to care for the little prince well. She never suspected. I suppose few would—if someone hands a baby to you, you don't look for a lie in the child's face. To my eyes the two babies were clearly different, but then I had nursed them both. If you saw them separately, with their fair hair and their dark eyes, only a few days apart in age, I suppose they did look very much alike.

In some ways it was strangely like the journey we had taken after we were first married. Spring had come early that year, and it was warm enough to sleep by the roadside, even for the baby. This time we had a packhorse from the king's stables, a gentle mare with a coat the color of just-turned earth. Myrddin said I should ride, to save my strength, but I felt queasy, perched so high above the ground, and I preferred to walk. Once again, Myrddin had his harp on his back, to prove his profession and grant us lodging and free passage wherever we went.

But on this journey, unlike that first one, Myrddin hardly spoke. He wasn't angry; he seemed to be thinking of something far away, hardly even noticing where he was putting his feet. And there was Arthur, wrapped in a sling I'd fashioned from my cloak, a warmth against my heart and a constant reminder of my worry for my own son. I had faith in Myrddin's promise, but that didn't keep the worry from growing.

Still, when we had stopped for the night, Myrddin would play his harp, for the sound seemed to soothe Arthur when he was restless. And I would dare to imagine what our lives might be like after we'd delivered Arthur into safekeeping. Myself, my husband, and my child all together, all safe, and far away from kings and their destinies.

We took our way at first toward my father's village. But when we were out of sight of Caerleon we turned south, walking over quiet, little-traveled roads. Finally I asked Myrddin where we were going.

He looked at me, a little surprised. Lately he seemed to forget I was there, noticing my presence only with a start. "A Roman town," he answered. "A few days' travel from here. There's a lord's family there, they've just lost their own son. They'll adopt Arthur."

"How do you know?" I stopped to pick a bramble out of the sole of my boot.

Myrddin's smile was thin and joyless. "I know."

I supposed I shouldn't have bothered to ask.

The town, of course, was where Myrddin had said it would be. The family he meant to raise Arthur lived a little apart from the rest, in an old Roman stone house surrounded by fields and orchards. In the end I told Myrddin to leave me behind. I thought I might not be able to make myself hand the baby over. He was not my own son, yet my arms felt terribly empty and light when Myrddin took him from me.

Myrddin returned after some time to find me crying silently. Without a word he put an arm around my shoulders, and I leaned against him as we made our way back to the road.

I never asked Myrddin what he had told this family to make them take in a stranger's child. What must they have thought of this tall, sober-eyed bard who arrived on their doorstep with a baby in his arms? But I knew well enough how persuasive Myrddin's absolute faith in his own visions could be. Faced with his rock-hard certainly that they *would* take the child, they probably had little choice.

Somehow the road back to Caerleon seemed much longer than the road away. I urged Myrddin to walk further every night, even rode sometimes, although it still made my stomach uneasy. Myrddin begged me to rest, but my impatience kept me from sleeping well even when we did at last stop for the night. My breasts were sore with too much milk, and my anxiety for Duach tore at me.

So we arrived back at Caerleon earlier than we expected. I ran to the nurse's house at once, but she was not there. Perhaps she had taken the baby to our chamber.

But only Olwen the midwife was in our room. She had a small square blanket in her hands and was folding it carefully. I had wrapped Duach in it just before we left.

"Nimue!" Olwen's face brightened with her smile. She ducked her head in respect to Myrddin. "Back so soon? And how is your father? Where's the little one?"

I remembered in time the lie we'd prepared. "A fever," I said as mournfully as I could when I was all but dancing with impatience to see my son. "It was very quick; he didn't suffer long."

"Oh, Nimue, I am sorry." Olwen laid the blanket down on the bed and came to embrace me. I felt a pang of guilt. All along I had been thinking about how hard it would be to deceive Uther; I'd never thought how it would feel to give false pain to someone I liked. "Such a grief for you," Olwen said sympathetically. "And he was so strong and healthy. I always had my fears about Arthur, but yours . . . "

Something seemed to have thickened my tongue, stiffened my jaw. It took me a few moments to speak. "Arthur?"

"Has no one told you?" Olwen drew back to look at me. "Then I am sorry again, my dear. I know you loved him too, just like your own."

I heard Myrddin's voice, as flat and distant as if he were in one of his visions. "What are you saying?"

"The little prince died, I'm afraid. He stopped breathing in the night. Some babies do. A great grief to us all . . ."

Her voice faded, and then another one crashed too loudly in my ears. "Nimue? Love? Are you all right?" Myrddin's face loomed over me. Somehow I was lying on the ground.

"You fell," Myrddin said softly, clumsily. "You fainted and fell on the ground. I couldn't catch you in time. Are you—"

"Murderer," I whispered, drawing back from him. There were other people in the room—had I screamed? Uther was there, beside the door, and people crowded behind him.

"Hush, love, hush, Nimue," Myrddin said firmly. He took my hands. From the burning heat of his skin I knew how cold my own must be.

Olwen knelt down beside me and put an arm around my shoulders. "You must be quiet now, Nimue," she said, very gently.

"He killed the child," I told her. "Uther killed him."

"I know." She leaned close enough so that no one else could hear her words. "And if you are not quiet now, they will kill you too."

I stared at her in incomprehension, and turned to the other faces in the room. "He murdered the baby!" I cried. "Killer at a court of murderers!" But it was at Myrddin, not Uther, that I looked.

They silenced me eventually, and Olwen poured something bitter down my throat to make me sleep. They kept me so for three days, trying to assure me when I woke that no one had murdered Arthur, and pouring drugged wine down my throat when my screams and accusations grew too wild.

On the fourth day I awoke calm. Olwen was asleep on a pallet beside my bed. Myrddin was nowhere to be seen. I rose silently and dressed, wrapped my cloak around me, and put my knife at my belt. There was no one stirring in the kitchen, so I found old bread and cheese and a flask of wine. I left Uther's court as the sun was rising, slipping out through a gap in the ruined wall.

It took me three weeks to walk to my father's house, begging food where I could along the way and sleeping by the roadside. I left all but my knife on the shore and swam the river, for there was no answer to my shouts. The house was empty, the garden grown wild. There was a smooth green mound by the river's side.

5

THE RIVER DOESN'T FLOW BACKWARD. But that's what I've done, returning here. I thought I would be safe, that I could forget all the sorrow my foolish longing to see the world had brought me.

My old friends couldn't understand why I refused to speak of the world beyond the river. They were even angry. That's when the names began. Madwoman. Crone. Witch.

Now they hardly speak to me at all, except to come in secret with their troubles, with cows gone dry and weeks without rain, with sickness and pain and useless husbands, and the young girls with their lonely loves. As if I were a prophet like Myrddin, or a priestess of the old days, as if I were something more than a lonely old woman who can hardly remember her only child's face.

I tell them I have no answers. But they still come back, begging me for wisdom I don't have.

Now and then I ask my visitors for news. At first they told me of Uther's wars, and finally of his death. And even worse wars as every king Uther had conquered fought for the empty throne.

Then they told me of a new young king who claimed the

Dragon's sword and took Caerleon for his own, defending it against every rebellious lord and greedy neighbor who thought a boy would be easy prey. It seemed they were wrong, for he won battle after battle, until there were whispers of witchcraft or unholy bargains. And to add to the confusion, he made allies of his defeated enemies instead of destroying them, slowly gathering the island into the kind of peace Myrddin had imagined.

When I heard of this new king, I left my home for the first and only time in all these years. The way was long, since there was no ferry and I had to walk to the nearest ford. When I arrived at last at the stone city, it was full of people, bright in their best clothes. I found I had come to court on the young king's marriage day.

The great hall was opened for a feast, for those lucky enough to push their way inside. I found my own way and looked into the hall.

There was the king at the high table: Arthur, whom I had rocked and nursed and tickled and soothed to sleep. He was fair-haired still, with Igrayne's dark eyes, turned on the new queen at his side. She had long hair the color of wheat fields in the afternoon sun, gathered simply to the back of her neck, and she was laughing at the young lord who stood by her side. Slight and slender, he was dark as a Roman, with black hair that slid into his eyes as he bent down to answer her.

Myrddin had let his beard grow longer. His hair had faded; I put a hand to my own braids, streaked with iron gray. He was speaking to Arthur, but he turned suddenly, his eyes scanning the crowd, and saw me.

I left the hall.

Alone, I took the long road back to the house that had been my father's and now was mine. One day not long after, at the fading of the light, Myrddin came to my door. Hesitantly he laid his hand against my cheek. "Nimue," he said softly. "My Lady of the Lake. You are still so beautiful."

We sat together by the fire, speaking very little. I asked him if Arthur would be everything he'd hoped.

"I play the harp very little now," Myrddin said. He spread his hands in front of him; the blue veins were swollen, the fingers stiff. "But Arthur will make a song, all of them together will make one. The land will be proud to say that once the great king walked it."

We said nothing else, and after a while Myrddin lay down to sleep. I waited, watching as the flames carved pale shapes out of the air.

I had let him have his king. The king he had sacrificed his own son for, the king he had lied to me to protect. He had lived long enough to see that king on the throne and to see the peace that had meant so much to him take root in the land and start to grow. I had let him have his king, and that seemed like mercy enough to me.

But strangely, as I took my knife in my hands, I didn't think of our son, or of the blood price Myrddin owed me. Even as I drew the blade across his throat, all I thought was, *Enough.*

Enough. Now leave him be.

I could not raise his mound myself. I wrapped him in his cloak and dragged his body to the tree he had said was holy, and laid him inside its hollow trunk. Carefully I closed his eyes.

I thought he and I would be at peace at last. But peace was never something Myrddin was good at.

Even now his bones still whisper to me. I dream of messages that are lost, of warnings not given. It was a cruel gift Myrddin had, and I never wanted any part of it. But maybe when his life's blood touched my hands, something of his vision passed to me.

Or maybe the things I see now are a punishment for my own guilt. For not speaking a warning to Igrayne when I could. For trusting too much in my husband's promise, not enough in my own doubts. For not seeing, as I had every chance to see, how blind Myrddin's visions could make him.

By the river yesterday I saw a young man, just grown out of boyhood. He was dressed as a warrior, in chain mail, with a drawn sword in one hand. He looked so much like Igrayne that it took my breath away.

He was muddy, bloodstained, stumbling with exhaustion. But

when he looked up, away from me, out over an empty field, his face filled with a hatred alight with joy. I thought he would murder like a saint prays, and with the same hope of blessing.

I remember what Myrddin once said: "*I saw them together, father and son. Each had a sword—*"

He never told me who would die.

Morgan

6

ARTHUR WAS MY GOLDEN BROTHER. He had thick fair hair and skin that kept a faint summer brownness even in the dead of winter. He drew my heart the way a candle in a dark room draws your eye, so you can see nothing else.

I WAS FOUR YEARS OLD when my father went to war with Uther Pendragon. I didn't understand most of what was happening, or maybe nobody told me. I only knew that my father was gone most of the time, that my mother was worried. But she would smile when she saw me looking at her. "Such old eyes, Morgan," she would say, stroking my hair, "in such a young face. Don't worry so—it will be all right."

Of course I believed her.

Until a night when I woke out of a dreamless sleep into a deep silence. My sister, Elen, older by two years, was curled up in the bed furs next to me and our nurse, Tannwen, slept in a corner, but I didn't want either of them; I wanted my mother. I squirmed out of the furs. The shock of the cold was like diving into a vast black lake. I couldn't hear my own breathing. The great hall, when I hurried across it, was as silent as if every sound had frozen.

A man was standing before the door to my parents' chamber. He seemed enormously tall; his dark cloak, wrapped around his thin shoulders, flapped and shuddered as he shrugged with impatience or cold, and as he shifted his weight from foot to foot. Light came through the cracks in the doorway behind him, and turned him into a black, winged shadow. I expected to hear him croak like the crows, or flap a few steps instead of walking.

I was sure this crow-man would swoop down on me and carry me away if he saw me. Carefully, I crept into the darkest shadows. When he moved a few steps away from the doorway, I ducked behind him into the room.

Candles were on the floor and chests, dimly burning. My father was lying on the bed, his head turned to one side. His eyes were half open. Something dark red, like wine, soaked the furs around him, splattered his face, his hair, stained the front of his white tunic.

Another man, one I didn't recognize, was standing beside the bed, fastening the buckle of a sword belt. There were red scratches on his face, and he rubbed them with the back of his hand. When he saw me, he drew in his breath angrily to shout.

My mother was sitting on the floor beside the bed, her skirt crumpled up above her knees. As the stranger's voice rose, she turned her head slowly. Her eyes were wide open, but they were as dull as my father's. There was blood on her mouth, and a puffy swelling around one eye. Her gaze slid over me without recognition and came to rest somewhere else, somewhere far away.

The stranger finished shouting: "Take her out of here!" I backed a few steps away from him and ran into the crow-man behind me. I heard him gasp, "Child, don't look," as he picked me up, holding me gently, though I kicked and hit at him. He did not have a crow's face after all, but a man's, thin and narrow with shaggy brown hair and anguished, dark blue eyes.

He carried me quickly away, and handed me to Tannwen as she came running wildly through the hall, dragging Elen behind her by one hand. I put my head down on Tannwen's shoulder, not wanting to see what sights went with the sounds I could hear— the harsh clang of metal, the dry cracking that was wood splitting open, angry shouting, sobs, screams.

Tannwen hurried us out to the dark courtyard, where there were a few torches lit, and people gathered around a cart and horse. She lifted Elen and me to the back of the cart and climbed in after us, wrapping us in the cloak someone handed up to her. I clung to her as the cart rattled out of the courtyard, leaving my mother and father alone in the room with the stranger and the crow-man, leaving them alone.

WEEKS LATER WE WERE IN ANOTHER DARK COURTYARD, lit by a few smoldering torches. Elen was asleep in the cart next to me. Tannwen had wrapped her cloak around both of us. I huddled against Elen for warmth, listening to Tannwen's voice come out of the dark.

"But you *have* to take them! Your own sister's children—"

"I've my own children to think of—"

"There's nowhere else for them to go."

"Doesn't their father have any relatives in the south? To come all this way . . . "

"But they couldn't stay in the south, my lady. It's not safe."

"Oh, very well, now that they're here. Igrayne was always so foolish. I warned her . . ."

Already Tannwen was lifting us down from the cart, setting Elen on her feet, carrying me as she followed a short, plump woman in a dark dress up narrow stairs and down dark hallways. The woman's voice drifted back to us. "I always had to look after Igrayne . . . she never thought about what she was doing . . ." She led us to a room with sleeping furs spread over the floor and a warm fire in the hearth. About a dozen women and girls were sleeping or combing their hair or sitting and talking by candlelight.

"They can sleep here tonight," the plump woman said, frowning a little. "Tomorrow we'll settle them elsewhere. Is this the oldest?"

"Yes, my lady, this is Elen," Tannwen said. She set me down and knelt to smooth Elen's hair. "And the little one is Morgan. Morgan, this is your mother's sister, your aunt Morgausa."

Morgausa smiled as she bent down to look at us. "Well, you're a pretty child," she said to Elen, her voice gentler than before. "Welcome now you're here, both of you." She would have touched my hair, but I shrank away from her, pressing closer to Tannwen. I'd already understood that she didn't want us here. I gave her an unfriendly look until her smile faded.

My aunt straightened up. "You'll stay here to take care of them?" she demanded of Tannwen.

Tannwen looked up in surprise. "No, my lady! I've my own family to go back to. Be good girls now, do as your aunt says," she told us, kissing us both in quick farewell and rising from her knees, her skirt brushing against me as she turned to go. My aunt followed her out of the room, objecting and complaining.

I was yawning, and Elen's eyes were closing where she stood, so some of the women gathered furs together to make a bed for us. Elen was asleep at once. I lay quietly, listening while the women gossiped—about us, what had happened to our parents, whether Morgausa and her husband would keep us—until one by one the candles were blown out. After a while my eyes started to ache from staring into the darkness. I let them shut for just a few seconds.

I think my screams roused half the court. Elen was rocking me in her arms, crooning soothing sounds in her throat. The women and girls crowded around our bed.

Suddenly my aunt was there, in a hastily pulled-on dress, her eyes wide with alarm. "What in the name of the good earth is all this? Who is making that horrible noise?"

"I think she's had a nightmare, my lady," one of the women offered.

My aunt stood by the bed, her mouth tight with suspicion. Suddenly she pulled me out of Elen's arms and gave me several sharp slaps across my face, ignoring Elen's wail of protest. "There'll be no more of this, do you hear? Spoiled, you are, just wanting attention. Look at her, not even crying," she appealed to the other women nearby.

It was true. Back in Elen's arms, my cheeks burning, I was

shaking so hard I could barely breathe. But I wasn't crying. My eyes felt as dry and sore as if sand had been poured into them.

Eventually I learned not to scream when I woke, night after night, from dreams in which crow-men carried me away while my mother looked serenely on. But even when I made no sound at all, Elen always knew when the nightmares had woken me. My sister rarely spoke, even to me, but she would hold me tightly until it felt safe to sleep again, sometimes softly humming one of our mother's songs.

The nightmare grew worse when, five years later, my aunt married Elen off shamefully young to the first man who would have her. After that I slept in the bed furs alone. But when the crow-man came to hunt me nearly every night, I taught myself to wake with a hand over my mouth, not to make a sound.

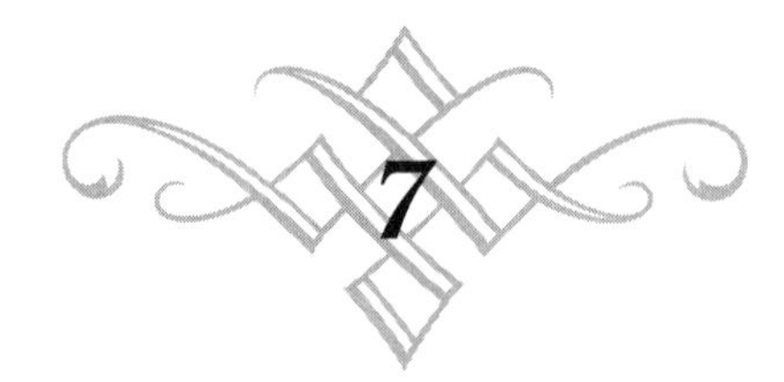

7

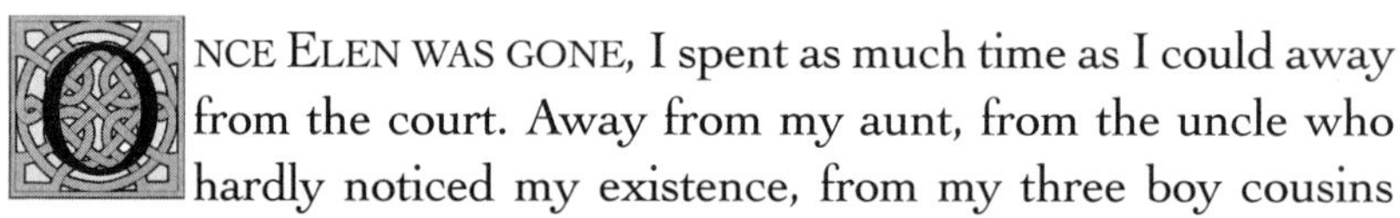

ONCE ELEN WAS GONE, I spent as much time as I could away from the court. Away from my aunt, from the uncle who hardly noticed my existence, from my three boy cousins and their scorn for girls and poor relations. I spent days out on the hills, in any kind of weather, exploring the woods and valleys and caves. I even made my way into the old stone-lined barrows, empty ever since the last of the old folk passed through them on their way to the shadow world. When I'd come back to the court to eat or sleep, people looked at me as if I were a ghost. Some made the cross or the old sign against evil as I walked by.

One wet day in early spring, ten years after I'd come to live in the north, I hurried down from the hills, carrying a stray lamb in my arms. The shepherds had asked me to look for it; I'd found their lost animals more than once before. I gave the lamb to one of the shepherd's boys and went to the kitchen. Wet and muddy and scratched raw by brambles, I pushed aside a few dogs and settled down by the fire, shutting out the clamor of cooks and serving boys behind me.

"Over there," I heard someone say as I reached out my hands to the blaze. One yellow flame leaped up, bright as a silk ribbon, and I let it brush my fingers. Strange how solid fire looks, when you can't feel its shape. How can something that feels like nothing, like air, cut as sharply as a knife?

"Morgan!" A hand shook my shoulder and I twisted around to push it away. Gawain, my oldest cousin, was glowering down at me. "You're daft, girl, you'll burn yourself again. Why don't you answer when I call you? My mother wants you."

"Morgausa never wants me," I disagreed. But just to prove me wrong, my aunt herself came bustling across the kitchen, scolding. "*There* you are, you little devil, filthy as ever, look at you!" I had on a pair of Gawain's old trousers and a patched tunic, much more practical than a skirt for crawling through brambles. "Go and clean up this instant, put on a dress for once, comb that rat's-nest hair of yours, and be ready for dinner."

My aunt didn't like to see me at the table; she usually let me forage for myself in the kitchen. "Why?" I asked lazily, not getting up. "Have you found a new suitor for me?" Morgausa should have known better than to try. I had scared off every man for miles around; I wasn't going to submit tamely to my sister's fate.

"A new suitor indeed! Who would have you? Look at you!" she fussed. "No, there's important news we have to tell you, so go and make yourself decent. And hurry!"

If I hadn't been curious I wouldn't have done it, since I made a point of never obeying Morgausa. But I wondered what *important* news she could have to tell me—she, who was usually glad to forget I existed. I didn't move until she'd left the kitchen, however, and I scrubbed my face and hands but didn't put on a dress or shoes. No need to humor her completely.

I saw that it wasn't just the family at the high table as I slipped into the last seat on the bench. There were my aunt and uncle and all three cousins, but also a thin quiet woman in a plain dress, who peered at me sharply from her end of the table. My aunt sighed as she saw me, and my youngest cousin Gereint nudged his brother Gwythr and giggled. I scowled at him.

"Mother Angharad," Morgausa said with an air of weary patience, as mutton stew, thick with grains and vegetables, was spooned into our bowls. I began eating hungrily. "This is my niece Morgan. We have spoken about her. We would like her to be taken into your abbey as a novice, and perhaps eventually to take vows."

I choked on a piece of turnip. Mother Angharad was looking doubtfully at me.

"She needs much training," Morgausa said regretfully as I coughed. "She is wild and unmaidenly, I regret to say, but under your teaching I am sure she will improve."

"I won't go!"

"Quiet, Morgan!" Morgausa glared at me. "Mother Angharad, we would like to give a gift to the abbey, in token of our gratitude for taking our niece."

"You can't make me go!"

"Sit down, Morgan!" That, of course, was enough to keep me standing.

"I'm not a Christian!" I yelped. It was true. I refused to be trapped in a stuffy church listening to incomprehensible Latin. Out on the hills, I felt myself much closer to the spirits of the forest and rivers and mountains, who sometimes listened to my prayers.

"You see how she needs instruction," Morgausa said to Mother Angharad, who looked as if she were rethinking the bargain.

"Maybe they'll teach you manners," Gawain suggested, grinning maliciously. I reached across the table and dumped a bowl of steaming mutton stew into his lap.

I hope my aunt and uncle gave the abbey a truly valuable gift to make up for the difficulty of being saddled with me. My uncle spoke to me for perhaps the second time in my life that night, and told me that I could go of my own will, or be transported bound in a horse litter, to be locked in a nun's cell until I agreed to stay.

Not that I took vows. I flatly refused, and the sisters found that they couldn't force a vocation on me. They might threaten and coax and even punish me, but I wouldn't tamely submit to beatings, and when they tried locking me up I found I preferred the solitude of my own thoughts to the endless Latin of church. After a while the sisters gave up, prayed over me diligently, and left me to myself.

There was only one woman in the abbey I found worth talking to. She was not a nun; the sisters kept her as they kept me—a sinner to be charitable to. Rhian was a wise woman, and she knew medicines and even some small spells. Now old and blind, she still knew plants by their feel and smell. I would bring her flowers and leaves that I found on the hillsides, and she would tell me their names and uses. She taught me what would make broken bones knit, what would help a woman deliver a baby safely or lose it from her womb before it formed, what would open the mind to visions from the gods, and what would kill a man.

In all my time at the abbey I heard nothing from my aunt until the day a message came ordering me home. Presumably Morgausa thought nine years should have tamed me at least a little, and wanted to offer me to another suitor or two. Although at twenty-three I was nearly too old for marriage, and, I hoped, not the least bit tamed.

Since I thought I knew the reason for my aunt's summons, I didn't bother to question the men Morgausa had sent to escort me. So I first knew that I was wrong about the new suitor when we rode into the courtyard and Gawain, hurrying by, recognized me and came to greet me.

"Cousin Morgan!" he called out, grinning at me. Much taller than I was, he had become a fine young warrior—at least he obviously thought so—with a spiky red mustache and a neatly cropped beard. "You look just the same. I see the good sisters haven't managed to teach you manners after all. A pity." I was tempted to rip his new mustache out by the roots. Instead I smiled at him.

"You're all grown up, cousin," I said sweetly. "What have you done to *earn* your beard?" He surprised me by bursting into laughter.

"Oh, you haven't changed! A—"

"A bitch like always," I agreed. But his laughter was almost friendly, and I found myself reluctantly relaxing.

"I'll show you to your chamber," he offered cheerfully, walking with me across the courtyard. "We're crowded to the rooftops here, but my mother saved you a room to yourself." No doubt, I thought sourly, Morgausa wanted to be sure that I had as little chance as possible to offend people. "Do you remember the house well? It's been a long time, I know."

I remembered it well enough to know that it had not always been this busy. There were kitchen servants rushing by carrying baskets piled high with warm loaves from the ovens and vegetables from the garden, horses hobbled and left to graze by the outer wall as if the stable were overflowing. Had my aunt found someone important to offer me to? "He must have brought many people with him," I commented.

"That he did! I don't know where we'll put everyone—he should have remembered we're just a poor northern kingdom, not one of those Roman towns down south. But not many warriors, I'll grant him that. He's bent on making a grand show of how much he trusts us."

"Why shouldn't he trust us?" Was I to be the bait in one of my uncle's alliances? I didn't like the idea.

"Oh, certainly, why shouldn't he?" Gawain seemed to think I was making a joke. "We're family after all. Of course we've spent the last three years at war with him, but he wants us to think that's all forgotten. He's a politician, your brother."

I stopped short in astonishment. "My *brother*? I don't have—oh." I smiled in comprehension. "Elen's husband, do you mean? She's here?" I asked eagerly.

But Gawain was staring blankly at me. "Not your sister, your brother! Didn't they tell you?" I shook my head. "Your brother, Uther Pendragon's son! The high king!"

"My brother? The king?" I sounded like a fool, and hated myself for it, and hated Gawain more for grinning as if my confusion were a grand joke. I wouldn't ask another question, I would find out from someone else. I wouldn't let him stand there and think me a fool.

But Gawain hadn't waited for a question; he was already talking. "Are you deaf, girl? King Arthur, the son of Uther Pendragon and the lady Igrayne, your mother, does that make it clear? He's here to make peace, and he wants to meet you—what's wrong with you? Morgan?"

I wouldn't answer. I let him walk me to my room, ignoring his questions, and shut the door on his persistence. There was a window in one wall, and I went to push the shutters open and sit down on the broad sill, staring out over the familiar hills.

"The lady Igrayne, your mother—"

I had not thought once of my mother in nineteen years.

I had not forgotten her, or any detail of the night when I had seen her last. Now that I looked back, I could see the memory, in sharp lines and clear colors, like an illumination in Mother Angharad's prayer book. But I had never once wondered what had become of her. In my mind she was like one of those tiny paintings, distant and removed and frozen in time. Locked forever in that room with my father's blood staining the bed furs, and the crow-man standing guard outside the door.

I was old enough now to know what my mother's bruised face meant, and my father's bloody stillness. Looking back, I was astonished at the things I knew about that night. Things the four-year-old child had seen and not understood, things the growing girl had heard and remembered without ever acknowledging.

My father had warred against Uther Pendragon, and the Pendragon and a few of his men had somehow crept into the castle. While his soldiers had opened the gates and let the Pendragon's warband in to slaughter the household, Uther had murdered my father in his bed and taken my mother to wife. And the crow-man—who was he? My newly awakened memory didn't want to supply me with this fact, and I was left with the memory of the tall man pacing nervously and seeming ready to rise in ungraceful flight.

Like everyone else, I had heard of Arthur ap Uther. I knew that his claim to Uther the Dragon's throne had been all that had stopped the southern kings from killing each other over it, since they had all determined on killing him instead. And I knew that after Arthur had beaten every southern lord into allegiance or alliance, my uncle and the northern kings had marched north against him—Gawain had said three years ago. Obviously they had lost. But somehow I had forgotten, or managed not to understand, that the Dragon's son was also my mother's son, my brother by half his blood.

8

ALL THE TORCHLIGHT IN THE HALL THAT NIGHT seemed concentrated in Arthur's face, his hair; he glowed golden, a sun god. His dark eyes, incongruous against his fair skin, were warm and bright. Eyes like mine, like my mother's. I grudged him those eyes, and his smile, the easy banter of his speech, his cheerfulness.

"Oh, I remember that!" Arthur's voice, his unrestrained laughter. "I stood on top of that hill and looked over your army, and thought it was about time for me to go home and become a monk, or take up shepherding, or some other trade."

I had combed out my travel-tangled hair until it lay smoothly over my shoulders. I had borrowed a dress from my aunt, pure white, so soft it clung to me as I moved, brushing every inch of my skin. But as I sat silently listening, I wished that I hadn't changed my clothes, that I'd stayed in my room or better yet at the abbey, that I'd never had to see this man, hear him ingratiatingly praise his former foes and make light of his own victories.

"You never would have taken us that day if it hadn't been for your horses." My uncle, serious and unsmiling. "The Romans used to fight on horseback, I know, but none of our kings have done so since the tribes of the old days."

"Oh, that was Owain here." Arthur slapped the shoulder of the man sitting next to him, a slight, dark man with a green and black brooch at his throat.

Owain didn't seem to see my uncle's cold glance. "The old tribes fought from chariots," he said in a low voice, leaning forward with his elbows on the table. "But chariots won't work in rough country like this. Men on horseback can maneuver more easily, and they're quicker. You can't put bowmen or spearmen on horseback, though."

"I hope my cousins will spend time at my court, and learn some of these new tactics." Arthur grinned. "Although I confess, it would take more courage than I have to put myself under Owain's teaching. He's a terrible bully. Once I saw him—"

Even my uncle was smiling; Gawain looked respectful; Gereint, nearly grown at fifteen, was openly worshipful. I sat unregarded, studying my brother. If there was nothing of his brutal father in him that I could see, there was also nothing of my mother's gentleness, her quiet strength. There was nothing in him at all—a courtier, a politician, playing the fool for my stupid aunt and her dour husband. Taking them all in. I pushed back the bench and stood. Gawain grabbed at my arm, but I shook him off.

Back in my room, I knelt before the window and folded my arms on the broad sill, laying my head down. The stone smelled damp and old, and was cool against my forehead and cheek. I felt, not the pain of a headache, but a soft, thick pressure building in my skull that made me want to scream, or beat my fists against something till they broke and bled.

When I heard footsteps behind me I didn't turn. There was the soft scuffling of leather boots against the floor, and no rustle of skirts. It would be Gawain then, sent by Morgausa to scold me back to the feast. If he didn't leave me alone—

"Lady Morgan?"

I turned at the unfamiliar voice and looked up into my brother's face. He held a candle, curling one hand around the flame so that all the room was in shadow except him. The gold of his hair and his skin glowed faintly against the dark.

"I was worried when you left the hall so suddenly," he said, putting the candle down on a chest. "Are you ill, my lady?"

I was sick, sick of him and the polite pretense that he was not the son of the man who had murdered my father—and yes, my mother too. I turned my face back to the window and ignored him, waiting for him to tire of my rudeness and go. He didn't go.

"I was glad to make this trip," he offered tentatively. "To meet my family over a table and not a battlefield. The Saxons are bad enough, but war with my own kin—"

I couldn't resist. "To hear you talk, you hardly managed to win any wars at all, and those only through pure luck," I said icily, without turning around. I wanted him to know that not all of the family had been taken in by his conciliatory jester's act. But he was amused, not offended.

"Oh, that? Well, if it makes them happy, why shouldn't I do it? If it can make peace between us, I'll swear that I won no battles at all, and all their men died of too much drinking and sleeping out in the rain. My pride's cheaper than blood. God knows we've spent enough of that already." For a moment his voice sounded tired and worn. Then the smooth courtier's tones came back. "And I was most pleased to meet you, my lady sister. I have foster brothers, but no sisters, and I have long hoped to know you, that we might be friends."

His arrogance infuriated me. *He* wanted to be friends? And what about what *I* wanted? But I kept my tongue between my teeth until I was sure of my voice. Then I spoke: "The sisters at the convent where I have been staying, my lord, say that this world is bound to disappoint all hopes."

He was shocked; I could feel that without looking at him. But Arthur had endless patience, and, as he had said before, very little pride. Now he tried again. "My lady, I know my father wronged your family."

You could call murder and treachery and rape a "wrong," I supposed, staring grimly out into the night. But it was not one he could mend with the blood price of his courtesy. Did he think his polite words would make me forget my father, lying unarmed in his blood? Or my mother, so lost in her desolation that she could not see her own child?

"But are you resolved on the blood feud, my lady?" Arthur continued. "I never knew my father, never knew that he *was* my father until after his death. How am I to blame for his crimes?"

I shook my head but didn't say what I was thinking: that he couldn't claim me as his sister through the mother we shared, and at the same time disown his father. He was the son of both.

Arthur came closer to the window. And when he spoke again, his voice was rougher, more awkward, more honest. "I take no pride in my father, Morgan, believe me. I inherited his throne, and all his wars, and I have been trying ever since to make peace, a peace that will not destroy us all . . . But I envy you, that you knew our mother. So many people have spoken to me about her, and they all loved her. What was she like?"

He was offering peace, I knew, trying once again to end his father's wars. I didn't answer, but this time it was not entirely out of stubborn anger. What was my mother like? My memory had frozen. All I could see was her lovely, stricken face turning slowly away from me.

Arthur came and sat on the windowsill, but he didn't look at me. "I never knew who my parents were," he said thoughtfully. "No one knew, not even my foster parents, except Myrddin, of course, and he would never tell me anything about them."

"Who's—Myrddin?" The question came out harsh and abrupt—but it was my first step toward Arthur's peace.

"He's—well, Myrddin is—he's hard to explain." I saw the white of his teeth as he laughed at his own struggle. "He was my father's court bard, and now he's mine—at least, that's what he does. Who he *is*—" Arthur shrugged. "He brought me to my foster parents, secretly, when I was just a baby. He used to visit from time to time. But he never told me anything until after Uther died. That night he came and told me who I was, and brought me Uther's sword. He fought half my battles for me, at first." Arthur shook his head. "You'll have to meet him, I can't tell you. He knew our mother, but he never speaks of her. He tells me all about my father, but never my mother. What was she like, Morgan?"

The second step. And I knew it, even while I tried so hard to remember that my hands shook. I pressed them flat against the windowsill. I could see her, sitting cross-legged on the floor, teaching Elen to play a game with string laced between her fingers. "She was very beautiful," I said slowly. "She would play with my sister and me, and laugh."

"It's so strange," Arthur said after a while, mostly to himself. "I grew up wondering who my parents were, and now I know. A family I never even knew, and half of them want to kill me for it." He seemed to feel that my silence, this time, was not hostile. Hesitantly, he reached out and laid his hand over mine. The warmth of his living flesh shocked my skin. I sat stock-still, but a shiver raced up and down my back.

Years ago I had tumbled out of bed into a cold black silence that had closed over my head like water. I had breathed in that cold until it froze inside me. Icy black splinters, sharp as broken slate, had filled my chest, invaded my heart, spread like frost through every vein.

With my blood frozen under my skin, I could hardly feel. I had stayed out on the hills in icy rain and bitter snowstorms and never felt cold; I had put my hands in the fire and not felt heat until my skin blistered. And I never cried, even when I woke shrieking from nightmares, even when they took my sister away. My tears had frozen too.

But Arthur's skin burned, as though it had trapped the warmth of the sun. As he let his hand rest on mine, the candlelight blurred, growing a deeper, richer orange that twisted and disappeared as tears thawed inside me and spilled down my cheeks.

ARTHUR CHARMED THEM ALL. My uncle approved of him, my cousins adored him; Gawain talked of nothing else than going south to Arthur's court. Morgausa treated him like a foster son, fussing over his wet clothes and his meals. Even the neighboring lords seemed to forget he was a southerner and a conqueror, and came to meet him and swear their loyalty without too much resentment.

"We *can* be strong enough if we stand together," Arthur argued, late one morning while we sat in the hall, the remains of a meal still laid out on the table. My uncle was scowling; the other northern lords he had invited as guests were listening doubtfully. Gawain was wide-eyed and worshipful. Owain was sitting apart, as usual, without a word to say. Like a black shadow cast by Arthur's brightness, he was always at his lord's heels, silent and watchful.

"Strong enough to defeat the Saxons?" one of the guests said doubtfully.

"Not strong enough to drive them from the island, maybe," Arthur conceded, "but strong enough to make a treaty and hold them to it. They can live south and east; there's good land there for them to settle—"

"Saxons aren't farmers," my uncle growled. "They'd rather slaughter a village than plow a field, and take what honest folk have made, their crops and stock and their daughters too."

"Would they?" Arthur considered. "They aren't just raiders anymore, uncle. They've settled already, they have farms and cows and sheep to tend. Farmers don't want to be off raiding villages; they want to be home watching their crops and thinking about rain."

"You can't be thinking of trusting Saxon savages, Arthur," my aunt scolded. "They'll knife you as soon as your back's turned—no, you *won't* get down till you've eaten every bite! Wasting good bread . . ." This was to Gareth, my youngest cousin, born three years earlier, while I was at the abbey. Now he whined and struggled on his mother's lap, whimpering to get down.

"But I am thinking of trusting them. Not right away perhaps—we need to show our strength first—but afterward . . ." Gareth squirmed free of my aunt's hold, crying with temper, and made straight for Arthur. He'd already learned that his tall cousin was the perfect refuge from any trouble.

Arthur laughed and swung the little boy up onto his knees. "All right, then, you can sit here if you're a good boy and finish what your mother gave you." He held out his hand for the crust of bread Gareth had scorned, and the little boy chewed happily as Arthur turned back to one of the guests who was speaking.

"But why should we rely on our strength alone? We can send to Rome for help."

"No. That I won't do." Arthur looked stern and, for the first time I had seen, almost like a king.

"It's been tried," Owain said, so softly he startled everybody. "Before my father's time, when the Saxons were destroying every town and village in the south."

"And Rome sent back word for them to defend themselves," Arthur said dangerously. "After centuries of taxes for their armies and tribute for their emperor, they couldn't spare a legion or two to help merchants and farmers. Well, we will defend ourselves. They may be surprised to see how well!"

"If you scorn the Romans so much," another lord said, with something like a sneer, "why do you keep your court in one of their cities? Are southerners so soft they need plaster walls and fires in every room?" A few of the guests laughed.

"I keep my father's court," Arthur said pleasantly, without a trace of offense. "I've been too busy these past three years to build a new one." His smile was guileless, but the silence stretched out a heartbeat too long.

Then Morgausa began scolding him for not finishing his meal. "As bad as that little devil there, you'll never grow up to your strength until you feed that gangling body of yours properly." She poured fresh ale into cups, and the tension slid away.

Arthur smiled at her, laying a slice of pale cheese over dark barley bread and biting down on it as she filled his cup. "I'm not a good example for my little cousin, am I?" he asked, bouncing his knee up and down to make Gareth laugh and clutch the table. "You're good to take care of me. I never had a mother, but I think I've found one now."

I'm sure they'd all forgotten me, as I sat at one end of the long table. But they turned when I dropped my wooden cup with a clatter, sending a flood of sweet cider rolling down the table to soak bread and cheese and hot meat pies.

I met the surprised faces with an angry glare. He could say that? After talking about my mother—*our* mother—he could say that to my stupid, fat, fussing aunt, mopping up my spill with the skirt of her apron and berating me for a clumsy fool? I was ready to hate Arthur all over again. But as he turned, I saw real contrition in his eyes. "Morgan," he said quickly, so low the others couldn't hear. "I'm sorry—"

"Moon-mad, I always said, or just plain half-witted, don't just sit there, Morgan, find some cloths and help!"

"I'm sorry," Arthur said again, his hand on my arm. And I would have forgiven him anything for the warmth of his skin against mine.

Morgausa cleaned up the mess, and the servants brought fresh food. Arthur's attention turned back to the guests. None of them noticed me as I slipped out of the hall, which suited me. I wanted no one's interference in the errand I had in mind.

Rhian had taught me what leaves and roots to mix, and what prayers to whisper, to bring a man to me. I'd only laughed, since there were no men at the abbey for me to enspell. And even if there were, I'd always thought that beauty was the most essential ingredient in such a charm, and the one I could never find no matter how hard I looked. But I still remembered what she'd told me.

I found my old path up to the bare crown of a hill that overlooked sweeps of rock-scattered fields. The fresh green of summer was gone; there was only dry stubble in the fields, and the bracken over the hillsides was the red-gold of polished bronze.

I had to stay out all afternoon to find what I needed. Back in my tower room, with dusk outside my window, I sent a boy to fetch me a candle and then burned the dry leaves and roots I'd gathered. The smell was faint and musty and sweet, but when I added a strand of my hair, the candle smoked and smelled sour, like something long dead and picked nearly clean.

That evening Arthur sought me out at supper and asked me if I would take him into the hills the next day. "They say you know them better than anyone else," he said, his eyes a little anxious, trying to make amends for the morning. I thanked Rhian in my heart that night before I slept.

Rhian hadn't taught me spells to control the weather. But the fickle northern sun came out and stayed out all day in spite of that, pouring warm gold over every stone and hill and tree. "I never knew the north was so beautiful," Arthur said, as we sat resting with our backs against sun-warmed stones, watching cloud shadows chase each other over the hills below.

Behind us was the tall ring stone. Set upright in the turf, it came up to my chin, with a hollow worn through the center by water or patient chiseling or ancient magic, big enough for a woman to lift her skirts and step through—and if she did, she'd conceive a child with the next man she chose. Couples from the court and village came here to be married if they didn't like the church or the priest; some did it both ways, to be on the safe side. I'd brought us here on purpose. It was an old place, and the old magic was strong in it.

"I can't believe you left all this to come south with me, Owain," Arthur added, glancing over at his pendragon.

"That's because you never lived through a northern winter," Owain said dryly. I hadn't been pleased, that morning, to find out he was going to accompany us. Arthur leaned back to look up at the sky, but Owain sat watchfully upright. "If it isn't snowing it's raining," he went on, "or both at once, and you don't see the sun for weeks on end. You'd never survive it."

"Southerners are soft, are they?" Arthur chuckled. "But this is beautiful, Morgan. It's enough to make me forget I'm a king. Or it would, if Owain didn't think he had to watch over me like I'm Gareth's age." He rolled his eyes at me, making us comrades in his affliction.

"Arthur," Owain said patiently. "It's not a joke. You may be charming them all over their food, but there are plenty up here who are still smarting from three years of defeat. Some of them would love to put a knife in your back."

"Or yours," Arthur reminded him. "They don't love you either." To me it sounded like an old argument on both sides. "I'd never have won if you hadn't come south to join me. And they know it."

"I didn't lose all my kin when I chose to be your pendragon,"

Owain answered. "They know I have people who'd avenge me."

Arthur shrugged off the disagreement and got to his feet, catching my hand to pull me up after him. "Come, Morgan, you promised to show me the old barrow here. Unless Owain thinks there might be assassins lurking inside?"

The entrance to the barrow was a doorway of stone built into the side of the hill, a lintel resting on two upright slabs. The opening between the stones was pure black, and Arthur hung back as I walked in. "Morgan, are you sure—" He stumbled down the two broad stone steps and came after me.

"Morgan, where are you?"

"Here." I held out my hand, felt him fumble and grasp it.

"It's dark as hell. Where are we going?"

"It turns here, be careful—"

"I can't see a thing—"

Holding his hand, I pulled him around the corner into the main room of the barrow. Rough stone walls curved up to meet the stone roof over our heads; Arthur's thick hair brushed against it as he stood cautiously upright. The builders had left a square hole in the ceiling, where a shaft reached up to the top of the hill, letting in faint sunshine to make Arthur's face stand out vividly against the dark stone.

He put up a hand to touch the stone roof gingerly. "We're *inside* the hill?" Even his whisper sounded weirdly loud, and made a shiver crawl over my skin. I was the only one who ever came this far into the barrow, and I never spoke out loud—why should I? I wondered if the last voices to echo off these walls had belonged to the old folk as they passed through, leaving this world forever.

Arthur was looking at me strangely; I realized I hadn't answered him. "I've never brought anyone here," I said softly, not whispering—the stones seemed to seize all the hisses and sighs of a whisper and fling them back. "I've never showed anyone—look at these!" The light was too dim for him to see the carvings, but I took his hand and placed the palm flat against the wall, letting him feel the ridges and curls and spirals cut into the stone.

"Amazing." His face was somber, but then suddenly lit by a wide smile. "Morgan, I have something to ask."

I nodded to show I was listening. But I was distracted by the feel of his hand beneath my own. I could feel every stiff hair, prickling against my fingers, the smooth skin beneath; I thought I could feel the pulse and flow of his blood under the skin. And then I thought I could hear it as well. The close walls of the barrow trapped the rush and throb of blood through his veins and echoed the sound back at me, louder and louder, until it was like ocean waves in my ears.

So I only understood part of what Arthur was saying. He was talking about alliances, and kin ties, and keeping the peace, the new peace he'd shed so much blood to make. And somehow he was talking about marriage, and how it would tie our family close together, and we were only half brother and sister after all, hardly more than cousins. And how it would do him, a southerner, good to have a northern girl as his queen, and it wouldn't hurt that my mother's family was of the blood of the old kings. He had brought his hand down from the wall and was holding mine tight; the rush of warmth up my arm made me dizzy.

"I know what my father did, Morgan. Myrddin won't talk about it, but enough other people have told me." In the faint light his face looked thin and young. I thought it was strange that he should look as if he were pleading for something from me. Wasn't he offering me a kingdom? "I'll make you happy, Morgan, I swear. If you'll forgive me, I'll make you happy." His other hand reached out to touch my cheek.

My face burned where he touched me. I wanted to slap his hand away. I wanted him never to touch me again.

"Morgan?"

I reached out for him, blindly pulling his face close to mine. I heard his muffled sound of surprise as my lips pressed against his. His hands on my skin were as hot as coals. My blood began to melt and run free through every vein.

Arthur promised me a great feast and marriage gifts when we returned to Caerleon. He wanted to be married in the north, however, to prove his point of family unity. North or south, I didn't care, but I'd had more than enough of priests and Latin. Two weeks after we sat together on the hill, we were married there in the shadow of the ring stone. Arthur paid my bride price in gold, filling my hands with rings and old Roman coins worn wafer thin, promising horses and cows as my own when we returned south.

Morgausa stood by with a stiffly disapproving face as my uncle gave Arthur my hand, and she was silent while all the rest of the court shouted and clapped as I stepped through the ring stone. Gawain was the loudest of all, wishing me a full belly and twins before the next planting. Once I would have been furious, but now I couldn't help laughing.

9

AERLEON, the old Roman town where Arthur lived, made my uncle's court look like a shepherd's hut. Arthur was watching me as we rode in; he saw my eyes widen at the great stone wall and the jumble of buildings inside it. "It's a ruin," he whispered cheerfully in my ear as we came to a stop in a stone courtyard and I slid off my horse into the curve of his arm. "Falling down on every side, we can't even keep the wall repaired. Who has the skill to build in stone like this now? But I won't keep court here forever." The confidence in his voice made pictures of even grander cities, walled hill forts, roads, towns, farms, mines, trading ships, roll in my head. Doubt seemed foolish—of course Arthur could make all this happen—and fear no more than a nightmare faded to nothing by dawn.

There was a confusion of people on every side, and Arthur was telling me names I instantly forgot while smiling faces went past. But I noticed how broad the smiles were—not just courtesy, but true delight that their king had found a wife, and utter confidence that any wife he chose would be the right one. I liked how they bowed their heads and kept them low in respect as they passed by me.

"Don't worry, I'll introduce them all again tomorrow," Arthur told me. "But here's someone you'll want to meet. Myrddin! I have news even you won't guess. I'm married!"

The crowd of people around us was thinning out, or perhaps I simply stopped noticing them. All my attention was caught by the man who came slowly forward to greet us. The late, low sun was behind him, turning him into a black shadow; his long cloak swung from his shoulders and swayed a little in the breeze.

"Myrddin, where have you been? This is Morgan, my wife." Arthur was grinning almost nervously. But his bard's quiet answer dashed him a little.

"Yes, I know." Myrddin turned his head and the light fell on his face. I saw the same narrow, dark blue eyes I had seen years ago, though the face around them was lined and the shaggy cap of hair touched with gray. I was startled by the grief in his face. He looked at me as if I were the ruin of all his hopes.

"Of course you know. Why did I ever think I could surprise you? Morgan, this is Myrddin, my bard, I told you about him. Morgan?"

The bard took a step forward to greet me. It was my old nightmare again: the crow-man swooping down on me, wings beating about my face, claws and beak ripping at my skin. He would carry me off, bleeding and helpless, to devour me. Only now it was not my mother looking calmly on. It was my husband, my golden brother, greeting the crow-man as a friend and welcoming him to my death.

I must have screamed. I think a great many people came running. And then my mind is confused, and I remember nothing clearly until I found myself lying warm in soft bed furs. I didn't want to wake up. I knew there was a great terror out there for me, but somehow I felt the dark behind my eyelids was safe. I lay still and listened.

"What can I do, Myrddin? Is she"—Arthur's voice was hushed—"mad, do you think?"

"Not more than the rest of us." Myrddin's voice was dry, even bitterly amused.

"But why should she take such a fit? I've never seen anyone—what can I do to help her?"

"You could kill her while she sleeps."

I was not afraid, or even shocked. The bard's tone was so calm and matter-of-fact that it seemed quite reasonable. Besides, I knew that the crow-man didn't want to kill me, not like that, with a knife to my throat or a pillow over my face. He wanted to carry me away, have me all to himself somewhere, where he could pick my bones.

Arthur's response was a wordless cry of protest. But as though he'd heard nothing, Myrddin continued. "But of course you won't. So there is nothing to be done. You've married your death, Arthur, that is all."

"Myrddin." Arthur breathed as though he'd run a race. "You didn't mean that."

"No," Myrddin said slowly, tired. "I didn't mean it. Dreams, my lord, that is all, I have been dreaming . . ." I heard the soft whisper of leather across the floor. "She looks like her mother, you know. Like your mother. I should go, she won't want me here when she wakes."

I felt Arthur's hand heavy on my hair, his anxious voice. "Morgan? Love? Are you awake?"

I shoved his hand aside, hard, and sat up so quickly my head swam. Arthur hovered over me. There were red scratches across his face; a few were bleeding. "I will not stay here," I told him.

He was too delighted to see me awake to listen. "Lie back, love, rest now. We've sent for one of the priests; he knows medicine—"

"I will not stay near that man!" I had to shout at him to make him stop smiling at me in that idiotic way. How could he act so concerned, my husband who had delivered me cheerfully into the hands of my worst nightmare? My fists clenched. But I forced myself to relax, to breathe. Perhaps, after all, he didn't know. He had promised to make me happy. He was a king. Kings must keep their word.

Carefully, I made my voice low and calm. "Arthur, you must do something for me." I clutched at the hand he lifted to brush the hair back from my face.

"Anything. Whatever you want."

"Kill him."

"Who?" He looked bewildered.

"Your bard. Myrddin."

Arthur sat very still. But the blood slowly drained away behind his golden skin, leaving his face a strange chalky gray. "Morgan," he said at last, speaking as though his mouth was stiff. "You don't mean that."

My blood felt cold in my veins. But I kept my eyes on Arthur's face, his warm hand in both of mine. "If you don't kill him, I'll leave. I'll leave, Arthur. Tomorrow."

"You don't know what you're saying, Morgan. You're sick. He's done nothing to hurt you—"

My breath caught on splintered ice trapped in my throat. "He is my enemy," I choked out. "I'll never stay where he is, Arthur, I swear—"

"Morgan, you never even saw him until today!"

"I saw him!" I wrenched my hands from his. "The night my parents died. The night—" I struggled to breathe. "When *your* father killed mine, and raped my mother, and took her away. He was there that night, Arthur. Ask him!"

Arthur looked sick with shock. He shook his head, helpless, silent.

"You have to kill him, Arthur. She was your mother too . . ."

Arthur hadn't stopped shaking his head. When he managed words at last, they were clumsy, stumbling against each other on their way out of his mouth. "Morgan. Even if it's true, I can't kill him. I can't kill a bard, you know that; it's against the old law."

"Then banish him. Send him away. Let him go to Ireland, to Rome, across the sea." I stopped. Arthur looked helpless.

"I can't. I—" He swallowed. "I need him, Morgan. I can't rule without him."

I NEVER EVEN UNPACKED MY CHESTS. Since I only had a few days to be high queen, I did my best at it, ordering servants to prepare horses and baggage and food for traveling with all the dignity and command I could muster. I suppose Arthur asked Myrddin about the truth of what happened the night he was conceived; I suppose Myrddin told him. After the first day Arthur stopped trying to argue with me. "Where are you going?" he asked as I stood in the courtyard, almost ready to depart.

"Home," I told him.

"Back north, to your aunt?"

"No," I said impatiently. "*Home.*" And when he still looked bewildered, I added, "Cornwall."

"But Morgan! Your parents' castle is deserted; it's been empty for years. You can't—"

I gave my attention to tying down a strap on one of my packs. My parents' ghosts would no doubt be better company than one of their murderers.

"Morgan." The loneliness in Arthur's voice unexpectedly touched me. He looked so young, my little brother, my lover, my husband. I thought distractedly that I was watching Arthur come to terms with the first peace he couldn't make. "I'd never have been king without Myrddin. He knows things no one else can. But I need you too. Morgan, please. Can't you forgive?"

Forgive him my father, his throat cut in the bed furs, my mother raped in his blood? I had been wrong to accept Arthur's peace. But it wasn't too late to take up the war again.

My parents were dead, my sister was gone, my brother and husband had allied himself with my enemy. I had no true kin, no one to stand with me. No matter. I would carry on the blood feud for as long as I was able.

Arthur *was* young. And somehow, the bloodied veteran of a thousand battles, he was also innocent. He had no idea that forgiveness would kill me. That only hatred was cold enough to keep the black ice that had become my heart from shattering into a thousand pieces.

I rode out of the courtyard without another word to him.

LUNED

10

THE FIRST TIME I SAW MY LADY ELEN was on her wedding day.

I was one of the crowd at the edge of the village waiting to see our lord Gormant bring home his new bride. There he was, riding among his warriors, laughing too loudly and probably a little drunk already. Behind him there was a shy-looking girl on a pony, with thin strands of her strange pale hair escaping from their braid to brush against her face.

She didn't even look my age, and I had only just reached my twelfth year. I passed her over twice, looking for the tall grown woman who must be the bride, until I realized that I knew all the rest of the company. If there was a bride among them, she must be the one.

Well. I wasn't the only one surprised, for around me I heard whispers and mutters, and saw frowns. "She's a child!" my mother said softly behind me. "Surely he won't take that poor little thing to wife."

I tried to imagine myself married, and couldn't. In a few years, of course, I'd have to think of it, marriage and children . . . but this girl was younger than I was, and Gormant nearly thirty.

I followed curiously as my mother and some of the other women led the girl to Gormant's chamber on the second floor of the tower. We had done our best to straighten it up, so the bed furs were beaten clean and the wooden floor was swept. Still, the girl's steps became more and more hesitant as she came up the stairs, and when she had gone a few paces into the room she stopped and looked as though nothing short of an earthquake would move her again.

Gormant loomed behind her in the doorway. Short and heavy, with his thick brown hair and bright red face, he looked a startling contrast to the frail, fey, frightened little thing he'd brought to wed. "Well, clean her up," he said to no one in particular. "Find her some fresh clothes. We'll be married in an hour, hurry." He pointed at me. "You—you'll wait on her." And with that tender leave-taking, he turned and rushed down the stairs as though on some urgent errand.

Why he chose me out of all the women and girls in the room I cannot say, for I'm sure he had no idea who I was. But that is how I was promoted from scrubwoman's daughter to handmaid, and how I began taking care of my lady Elen.

For as the other women bustled about, fetching clothes and water and soap and towels, Elen stood stock-still, with her head down, staring at the floor. When I came closer, I could see her trembling. As if she were my little sister, I put my arm around her. Her dark frightened eyes, odd and out of place in that pale face, fixed themselves on mine. "It's all right," I told her, unwisely promising. "It's all right, I'll take care of you."

Such a lie as was never spoken. How could anything be all right for this child, married to a man like Gormant?

Perhaps it was ungrateful of me to hate him. He may have been nothing more than a wandering soldier looking for a warband to join when he came upon our village four years ago. But he did know which end of a sword to pick up, which, as my mother said, was more than any of our men could claim.

He taught swordcraft to the men who wanted to learn, and hired enough warriors, many of them his own kin, to keep us safe from Pictish raiders and Saxon warbands. He even made us rebuild the old abandoned tower, and it was big enough to shelter us all, people and pigs and cattle and sheep alike, when raiding parties came. Now we no longer lost folk like we had my father, his skull split open by a Pict's axe before I learned to walk, or my younger sister, stolen as a slave when I was seven. And now that we could protect our stock, we had fewer hungry winters.

Which isn't to say I loved Gormant. None of us did. When we'd asked him to stay, few of us had bargained on a full warband we'd have to feed and clothe. And none of us had bargained on Gormant's temper. It didn't take him long to forget he was only a traveling warrior and set himself up as a lord. If he thought we were failing in gratitude, he was quick to remind us who we owed for our new safety. Anything at all could set him in a rage, and then he was free with his fists and vicious with his tongue.

But no one was bold enough to complain to Gormant's face, or even grumble loud enough for one of his cousins in the warband to overhear. My mother and some of the other widows took over the tasks of cooking and cleaning and sewing for Gormant and his men. And we all worked a little harder so there would be food enough, since we knew it wouldn't be Gormant and his men who would go hungry if we ran short.

So even as I made that rash promise I knew that nothing would be all right with Elen. I heard some of the women whispering that she was well-born and her family was powerful. They all thought that was why Gormant had chosen her. But I was with her after the feast that night, when Gormant came up to his new bride, and I knew there was more to it than power or politics.

I had combed Elen's fine hair smooth and helped her off with her white wool dress. With her fair skin and her glimmering hair, and her dark eyes swallowing up half of her thin face, she looked like a ghost or a spirit against the dark stones of the tower walls.

Gormant must have stood for some time in the doorway, watching her. Then his boot heel scraped against the step and she turned like a startled deer. He never looked away from her; I don't think he even knew I was in the room. "It's all right," he said softly, slurring the words, as if she were a dog or a horse he could soothe with his voice. I smelled mead and ale and sweat and wood smoke as he moved past me. "Don't be afraid," he was whispering as he reached out to touch a strand of pale hair that hung by her cheek.

But he was far too drunk to be gentle with her, and Elen was far too frightened for it to matter that he tried. I threw the dress to the floor and rushed headlong down the stairs and out through the hall where a few determined revelers were still singing by the fire.

When I crept home, my mother saw the tears on my face and took me in her arms. "They're not all like that, you know," she said, rocking me gently while I cried. "Your father wasn't, bless him." She sighed, blinking back tears of her own. "He wants you to look after her?" I nodded with my head against her shoulder. "Then you do a good job," she told me firmly. "She'll need it, poor little thing."

I was always good at taking care of things. The orphaned lambs I raised grew up strong and healthy; my little cousins always minded what I told them to do. Elen, it seemed to me, was just another of these—frightened and sick like a motherless lamb, lonely and uncertain as a child away from home. Soon it almost felt as if Elen were the little sister I had lost. And for her part, she clung to me from the beginning as if I were her true kin.

One day after Elen and Gormant had been married a few months, she and I were talking together in the tower room. The light from the window brushed Elen's hair, so fair it almost burned, like winter grass in the sun. I was winding up the skein of yarn I had been spinning; Elen was sitting on the floor with one of the hunting dogs sprawled beside her, his rough gray head in her lap.

"There were two new lambs born last night," I was telling her. "Both lively and well. And Bron's little boy is starting to walk." Elen smiled as she scratched behind the dog's ears; he closed his eyes and sighed with pleasure.

"And Cei says there's a storm coming, so he isn't going hunting tomorrow with the men—"

Elen sat suddenly upright, listening. I stopped talking as we both heard footsteps on the stairs. Quickly I gathered up my wool and slipped into the darkest corner of the room. Gormant was less likely to notice me there and order me away.

Elen sat perfectly still, looking at the floor, as Gormant came into the room. He stood for several moments, frowning. She didn't look up or stir, but only stiffened as he walked across the room. He nudged the dog in the ribs with his toe, not gently, and it scrambled out of the way.

"Here, for you," he said, and he let something fall in her lap. It was small—I couldn't see what it was—and it landed heavily on the soft folds of her skirt. Elen didn't move a hand to pick it up.

"There's no pleasing you!" Gormant burst out. Elen flinched, but he only turned and marched out of the room. By the doorway he paused. "You'll wear that," he said angrily, and continued down the stairs.

Once he was gone I went to Elen's side and lifted Gormant's gift from her skirts. It was a ring, a bead of amber several shades darker than Elen's hair, set in a band of gold. A lovely thing. What had Gormant traded for it? More, I thought, than he could properly afford.

I put my arm around her shoulders, holding her until she stopped shaking. The dog came to sniff at her ear with his cold nose and whine a little in his throat.

Elen and I both knew it was likely to be a bad night for her. It always was, when one of Gormant's gifts had failed to please his wife.

My failure to keep my promise to her was always bitter in my throat at times like these. I'd told her I would take care of her, and I couldn't do it. I could comb her hair, mend her dresses, see that she ate, hold her while she cried, homesick, for the sister she'd left behind. But I couldn't do a thing to protect her from Gormant.

I made another promise then, not aloud to Elen but to myself. I couldn't save her from her husband, but I would do my best to see that nothing else, and especially no other man, would hurt her.

So I was not just Elen's servant. I was her protector. When the village folk thought she was simpleminded because she was too shy to speak, I set them right. When she shuddered and grew pale if any man came near—even someone as harmless as Cei the blacksmith's boy—I made sure to be by her side. And as she grew quieter over the years, I became her voice.

I'd hoped things might get better between Elen and her husband as she became more a woman, less a child. But if anything they worsened. With each year she grew more beautiful, and with each year Gormant grew angrier, furious that she was always silent in his presence and sickened at his touch.

For eighteen years they were married. Each year Elen spoke less and less, and Gormant drank more and more, and I wove and mended and cleaned and kept one eye on the kitchens and the other on the fields, and wished there were some way I could set Elen free. But I could see none. At first Gormant had hated it that nothing he could do would please his wife. Soon enough he hated her for making him feel a brute and a fool. When Gormant couldn't make Elen smile he hit her, and climbed on top of her in bed at night as if he could destroy whatever it was that kept his heart in her unwilling grasp.

11

AS IT TURNED OUT, it was someone else entirely who set Elen free.

The first I knew about it was the commotion outside. I was braiding Elen's hair, and she turned her head to look up at me in question—it wasn't her way to ask when a glance or a gesture would do. Just then Bronwen, one of the servingwomen, put her head in the door, flustered and out of breath.

"Oh, Luned, it's—oh, I'm sorry, my lady—oh, Luned, come quick, what's to be done? They're bringing him in now, and where will we put him?"

Somehow, in all this time I'd been looking after Elen, people had gotten into the habit of bringing their questions to me. At first it was only simple matters—what dress Elen would wear. What food she liked. But as we both grew older, it came to be more than that. After all, the village folk expected someone to decide what we would serve a guest for dinner, or if we should harvest the barley early while the good weather held, or if the stores of salt pork would last the winter. How could Elen have done it, too shy to speak as she often was? As for Gormant—he was no farmer, and most often wouldn't be bothered.

Sometimes I would say I was speaking for Elen, but as time went by people came to act as if I had a true right to tell them what to do. And often enough they did it. Now Bron stood looking at me in a panic, wringing her skirt between her hands. It didn't seem likely that I'd get any sense out of her soon, so I tied off Elen's hair with a scrap of wool and promised I'd be back soon with the news, whatever it was.

Following Bron outside, I saw four or five of Gormant's warriors riding in. A stranger was with them, his hands bound behind his back. I got a good look at him as they pulled him off his horse. Slight and slender, dark like most northern men, he would have been handsome if he hadn't been scowling and covered from head to foot with mud. Behind him, another man's body lay over the back of a horse, with a thatch of red-brown hair and arms that hung limply down.

I stared as Bron clutched my arm, wailing in my ear, "I told you, I told you, and where will we put him?" I knew the hair, and the green trim on the tunic that I'd woven myself. For an instant I thought he might be only hurt, but if that was so his men would be taking him down and shouting for help. No, they simply let him lie there and huddled together, looking embarrassed.

Gormant dead—Mother Don and every saint help us. I was too surprised to decide if this was a blessing or a curse. Had the handsome stranger killed him? And how soon could we find a priest to bless the body? And above all, what would happen to Elen now—and to all of us?

"We'll put him in the hall, of course," I answered Bronwen sharply. "Where else is there? Call Morfudd and Cigfa, we'll have to clean him up. What's to be done with *him*?"

I asked the question of Siawn, the captain of Gormant's warband, who stood among the warriors, frowning like a priest at a Midsummer festival. His right sleeve was rolled up and there was a bloody rag tied tightly around his upper arm. He turned to face the prisoner, who was still held tightly by three men, as if he'd run off and shame them all by escaping, even bound as he was. Siawn put a hand on his long knife and smiled—that, with his black and yellow teeth, was a sight to strike fear into anyone.

"Cut his throat here, that's what," he answered without looking at me. "Where everybody can see it done."

The stranger didn't say a word. He only stood breathing heavily and glaring.

Most of the village folk feared Siawn more than Gormant—and with fair reason. Where Gormant would lash out with a fist when he was angry, Siawn was far likelier to use a knife. But once I saw the way he looked at Elen when Gormant was too drunk to notice, I'd been at pains to let him know he didn't frighten me. Oddly enough, it was Gormant himself who gave me the safety to be so free with my tongue—Siawn and all the rest of the men knew that if they harmed me, Elen would grieve, and Gormant would have the hide of anyone reckless enough to displease his wife. That was a privilege he reserved to himself alone.

And now that Gormant no longer stood between us, it was no time to start showing fear. "What, did you drag him all the way here just to cut his throat?" I asked, loud enough for everyone to hear me. Whatever the man had done, I didn't care for the idea of watching Siawn kill him like a pig at a butchering. "You could have done that in the forest. Take him to the cell, let him wait there awhile."

Siawn turned and narrowed his eyes at me. "Who said you could give the orders here? Serving wench!"

"Nothing should be done until our lord is laid out properly!" I snapped back. "Will you leave him hanging over a horse while you go about your butchering? Take him down, some of you, bring him to the hall." I turned away, hoping they wouldn't knife the stranger behind my back. But they were not all so hot for killing as Siawn, or they would have left him dead in the forest. Some of the men pulled Gormant's body off his horse and Cei, one of the warband, clamped one huge hand around the prisoner's arm and hauled him away.

Why I tried so hard to keep him alive I hardly knew. I wanted to know the truth of what had happened to Gormant, I suppose, and it seemed like a reckless thing to go killing the only witness before I had a chance to talk with him. And then I didn't grieve for Gormant, and felt a little gratitude to the man who'd struck him down, even if that man turned out to be a common highway thief.

Or maybe it was only that he had such a handsome throat, it seemed a pity to spoil it.

But the truth is, I think I already knew that a time had come when I'd need all the allies I could gather. And even a murderer, bound and in prison, might turn out to be an ally worth having.

Elen had never borne Gormant a son. And Gormant never named any of his other kin as an heir. But he had cousins enough in his warband, and of them Siawn was the closest, his father's sister's son. Some might argue that made Siawn our new lord.

Not if I had anything to say about it.

When I told Elen that Gormant was dead, you could hardly say she was grieved. Someone else might have thought she hadn't heard, or understood, but I knew my lady too well for that. She only breathed in, and opened her lips as if her new freedom were something to taste. And then closed them again as her new danger, too, came home to her.

"You should see him," I told her. "They'll think it strange if you don't. Only a minute or two, that's all. I'll go with you."

We walked down to the hall together. Bronwen and Cigfa and Morfudd had set up a table for Gormant and were washing him clean. His dirty clothing, sticky with mud and dark, drying blood, lay in a heap on the floor. The skin on his chest was ripped open like an old tunic carelessly torn.

Elen only stood by his head for a minute, watching his face. She had courage, for all her shyness. She stood rock still as she looked on him, and then turned to me.

"What will we do now, Luned?"

What could I answer? Bad as Gormant had been, Siawn would be worse, and we both knew he might easily have it in mind to marry her, to give himself more claim to Gormant's place. "You go back and wait for me," I said at last. "I want to talk to someone."

But before she left, I asked her for the ring Gormant had given her so long ago. She worked it off her finger and handed it to me, wondering but without questions.

The "cell" was really too grand a name for the place where they had stowed the prisoner. It was just a hole in the ground lined with stone slabs and roofed with turf over wooden beams. We used it to store apples and grain, turnips and onions, heads of cabbage and barrels of ale and mead.

There was a heavy trapdoor over the old stone stairs to keep squirrels and badgers out. Sometimes the men threw a thief in, or a cattle raider, and kept him there until compensation had been paid.

So it was hardly a formidable prison, and when I rounded the corner I saw that Siawn had had the sense to leave a guard. Cei was sitting on the edge of the trapdoor, whittling a stick down to a pile of shavings between his feet.

"It's damned boring out here, girl. Aren't you kind to come and chat with me." Cei grinned and made space for me on the trapdoor. A good thing it was Cei and not Alun or some of Gormant's other kin. Cei was village folk, one of us. The muscles he'd built swinging a blacksmith's hammer all those years had made Gormant claim him for the warband. But Cei never really liked carrying a sword as much as he liked pounding out plowshares and cooking pots on his anvil.

"What's going on in there?" he asked me. "I heard that fool Bronwen yowling. What's she crying for?"

I rolled my eyes. "Warriors die and women weep—isn't that what the bards say? What happened, Cei?"

Cei shrugged. "Damned if I know. He'd ridden on ahead of us somewhere. We could hear him crashing about, so we knew we could follow later, and even if he did fall off there'd be no harm done. He's used to it—and the horse should be too, by this time." He snorted and then went suddenly solemn, as though Gormant's ghost might rise up to curse him for laughing at the dead.

"Was he drunk?"

"Never more so. I think he was afraid to sober up in case the hangover killed him. But then we lost track of him altogether. While we were looking we heard yelling and steel crashing." Cei shook his head, frowning down at the stick in his hands. He'd whittled it down to a point already and his knife only sliced it sharper with every cut. "When we came on them Gormant was already dead. The stranger was just pulling the sword out of his ribs."

It was less information than I'd hoped for. But something he'd said caught my attention.

"He had a sword? The stranger?" Cei nodded. No common highway thief then. And as I thought back on his good wool and leather clothing and his angry pride, it didn't seem likely that he thieved for a living.

"What was the quarrel about?"

Cei shrugged again. "No one knows. He put up a good fight—Siawn's hurt and Dafydd and Hywel. But there were ten of us. And once we had him bound, he's not said a word, though Siawn threatened to cut his throat right there."

"Well then," I said thoughtfully. "I guess I'll have to see the prisoner and ask him myself."

"Oh indeed?" Cei looked up at me. "And maybe if you answer my question I'll let you."

It was an old joke between us. I was nearly old enough to be a grandmother, and Cei's wife was dead in her grave and their baby with her, when Cei had first asked me to marry him. Of course he was mocking me. So I'd made a joke of it, telling him I'd answer him when the harvest was in, or the new year had come, or the next time a flock of geese crossed against the full moon. Solemnly Cei would wait until the day I'd named had passed, and then he would ask me again.

But this was hardly the time for jokes, now when our lives might be toppling down around our ears. Impatiently I stood, putting my hands on my hips in disbelief. "Do you think I've time to think about you now? I've a few other things on my mind." Like what was to become of Elen, and of us all. "Are you going to get up off that door?"

Cei frowned, his knife pausing on the wood. "Siawn didn't say I was to let anybody in."

"Siawn isn't lord here yet!" I snapped. "Elen sent me, so move your fat rump off that door before you break it in and the prisoner escapes, and what will Siawn say to you then?"

Cei threw back his head and laughed. "Girl, you've got a tongue on you worth a bard's! Go on, then." He got up off the trapdoor and gestured me toward it. "I'll be here in case he tries anything. Just you scream." He heaved the door open for me and watched me down the steps, then shut it behind me.

Enough light fell through the cracks between the boards to let me see the casks of ale and wicker baskets of grain and dried herbs hanging in bristly bunches from the pegs in the ceiling beams. But I couldn't see the prisoner. I knew he must be back in the shadows, and suddenly I thought what a fool I was to stand defenseless before a murderer. I opened my mouth to scream for Cei when a voice came sharp and menacing out of the darkness.

"Tell your men that if they kill me, they'll have my kin down on their land like a wolf in winter. There won't be a building left standing, their women will be sold, and their sons will be slaughtered. I'll pay the blood price for that man's death, but there won't be a soul left to mourn in this miserable village if they dare shed my blood!"

So he had a tongue after all. I took a quick breath to make sure my voice wouldn't shake. "I'll tell them that, certainly," I agreed. "But don't you want me to cut your hands free first?" There was a long pause while I could hear him breathing. "Come into the light," I added, and drew my knife.

Slowly he stepped out under the trapdoor. In the thin stripes of light that fell across his face, I could see his dark eyes, narrow and suspicious. A bruise was turning purple over one cheekbone. After a moment he turned his back, and I cut the tight leather thongs around his wrists.

He turned and stood rubbing his hands together. Suddenly, quicker than I could move, he reached out and laid a hand over the hilt of my knife. But he didn't wrench it from my hand. "Didn't they tell you," he said, half threatening, half puzzled, "not to let a knife come into a prisoner's hands?"

"Didn't they tell you you'd be a fool to kill the only friend you have here?" I answered, without moving an inch. Slowly he withdrew his hand. I suppose he thought he could take the knife any time he wanted. Which was no doubt true.

"You're the one who kept them from killing me," he said, studying my face. "Why are you my friend?"

"I want something from you."

"Do you now." His mouth twitched in grim amusement. "You can walk above ground free as the air, so what do you want from a captive with his throat about to be cut?"

"Will you bargain?" I sat myself down, businesslike, on a cask of ale and gestured for him to do likewise.

He did so, looking bewildered and amused and resentful all at once. "I'll hear your trade. What can you want from me?"

As my eyes became more used to the faint light, I could see him fairly well. A thin, clean-shaven bronze face, high cheekbones, straight eyebrows with a quizzical tilt over dark eyes. His muddy, wet tunic was of soft gray wool, and the trimming was red and blue. It looked rich and fine, and completely out of place against a background of turnips and apples and ale casks. He raised a hand to his face and tried to rub some of the dried mud away. *Vanity?* I thought, much encouraged.

"Well?" he said, tired of my scrutiny. "What's your bargain?"

"I want you to marry someone."

His eyebrows all but disappeared under the fringe of black hair. "You want me to—what?"

"To marry someone."

The thin mouth opened in an incredulous smile. I, however, was deadly serious and I wanted him to know it. I leaned forward and scowled at him. He stopped smiling. "You mean it?"

"Would I sit here locked in a root cellar if I didn't mean it?" I snapped, out of patience.

"Well, but who—" I had him looking foolish, and I was glad of it. It meant he would be off balance, and listening to me.

"My lady." It didn't enlighten him, so I added, "The woman whose husband you killed."

I thought the cask would go over backward, he stood up so quickly. "You want me to *marry*— "

"Yes!" I said sharply. "It won't be so difficult. We'll find a priest, there's a monastery nearby, or we can do it with mistletoe and the old vows, if you prefer. But she must have a husband, and soon. Or are you married already?"

"No. No, I'm not—married." He began to pace about restlessly. Not that the cellar was big enough for it—every two steps brought him face to face with a wall or a basket of turnips. "You don't know anything about me! I'm a murderer, a highway thief, or a Saxon spy, for all you know. Do you care so little for your lady?"

"I know what I need to know about you."

"And what's that?"

"That you killed him."

That brought him up short. Before he'd been so caught by the ridiculousness of the thing—that he should be sitting in a root cellar listening to a serving woman propose he marry the widow of a man he'd just killed—that he was hardly listening. Now he was looking at me seriously at last, and came to sit back down.

"Am I supposed to be like a chieftain of the old days, or a Saxon brute, and carry away my enemy's woman over my shoulder? With her husband's blood on my hands, I don't see why either you or she would want this."

"Then you're blind!" I could have screamed in exasperation. "But if you'll listen, I'll explain. My lord left no son. He never named an heir. But his closest cousin is the man who would have cut your throat just now if I had not stepped in. And before I see my lady married to him— " Well, I wouldn't let it happen, that was all. "Has the light dawned?"

He sat still for a few moments, and then nodded.

"And," I added, more calmly, "I do know a few things about you."

"You do?" He looked almost alarmed. "What do you know?"

"I know that tunic wasn't woven in a farmer's hut. I know you're wealthy enough to wear a sword." Strangely, he looked a little relieved. What had he thought I was going to say? "And I know you can fight." It might not take much swordcraft to kill

Gormant when he was blind drunk, but anyone who could do that and then wound three other warriors without taking a scratch himself—I was willing to bet something on his skill.

"They're going to kill you, you know," I told him. "Siawn has to, you made him look such a fool, killing off his lord right under his nose. They only dragged you back here to do it where everybody could see. But if you marry my lady, you can make a claim for the lordship yourself." And maybe he'd only have to kill Siawn to get it. I didn't want a bloodbath on my conscience just to keep my lady safe. I took a breath. "So. Will you do it?"

All this time his face had been curiously blank while he listened to me. Now he hesitated, and spoke slowly, as if his tongue were a great weight in his mouth. "I—am not free."

All my heart, all my hope had been pitched to hear the word *yes* from his lips. Suddenly now I was floundering in disappointment. "You said you had no wife!"

"I do not. But there is one I . . . love." He was looking down at his hands now.

"You're betrothed?"

"No. She is not—we are not free to wed."

There was firm ground under me again, and I began to tread cautiously. "Not free? Is she married then?" He was quiet a moment, and then nodded. "Then why shouldn't you be married too?" I cried. It seemed entirely reasonable. He shook his head, but I pressed on. "I haven't asked you to love her! Marry her, protect her, and you are free to love anyone you choose." I didn't add that Elen would be more than happy if he never came near her bed—a man like this was probably not used to hearing such a thing, and would likely take the simple truth as an insult. "Appoint someone you trust to oversee things here—*I* can manage the women's side of things!—and you can go back to your love. Why not?"

He looked displeased with having his noble determination to die rather than betray his ladylove tossed aside so lightly. I poured words on him, as if I could melt him like spring ice in the river. "This marriage can be nothing more than politics—for show. Give Elen the protection of your sword, and you're free to go to anyone's bed you please, no one here will mind—"

"I have never done so!" I had misstepped badly, for he was towering over me, furious. "Keep your tongue off my lady's name! Or I swear—"

No time to be frightened now, I scrambled to recover. "Well then, what would it matter? If the love between you is so pure, what harm could it do if you were another woman's husband, just as she is another man's wife? Wouldn't you be even safer from sin, if you were both bound by oath to others?"

He turned away, and I found that I had run dry of words. I only sat upright, my breath trembling and fluttering against my ribs, waiting for his answer.

"You can twist words like a priest, or even a druid." He rubbed a hand over his face. "I might as well argue with a snake!"

"All my words come to this in the end," I said at last, quietly. "You'll be no good to your lover with your throat cut, and that's what they will do to you. If you want to return to her, you'll have to make your way out of this prison. And the only way to do that is to marry my lady."

He stood still for a while, and I think my heart must have stood still as well—certainly I would have heard it otherwise in that silence. At last he came back and sat down again, with a sigh that seemed to tear his very soul out by the roots. "You make a good bargain. I will marry her."

"And keep her safe?"

"I swear it."

I smiled, well satisfied. Quickly I handed him Elen's ring. "For a pledge," I told him. "Everyone here knows that ring, and it may protect you if—if I don't come back in time." He didn't look too pleased with the idea of depending on a woman's protection, so I hurried on to another question before he could object. "And may I know your name, who are to be my new lord?"

"Owain ap Urien, of Rheged."

I must have looked utterly foolish in my surprise, for even in his despondency he let out a brief laugh. "I've struck you dumb, maiden! And they say these are no longer the days of miracles."

"Owain of Rheged?" I repeated stupidly. Great Rheged is less than a day's ride to the east; some even say our village is on

Rheged's lands, although Gormant would never hear of it. But to find myself speaking to Rheged's young lord was not the only reason I was gaping. "Arthur ap Uther's pendragon?"

"The same." His face still wore a dry smile. "You see why I wouldn't tell your men outside who I am. After your lord tried to take my head off when I mentioned Arthur's name, I thought it would be best to keep silent."

If I had shocked him into idiocy before, he had his fair revenge now. I was speechless. The lords and kings here in the north certainly didn't care much for Arthur ap Uther, with his habit of gobbling up other people's kingdoms—all in the name of strength and unity against the Saxons, of course. Gormant in particular, hanging on to his tiny patch of land with his teeth and fingernails, hated Arthur. But he would start shouting with rage and waving a sword if anyone mentioned Owain of Rheged, who had not only given up the war against Arthur but had knelt at the conqueror's feet to serve as his pendragon.

Well, I had too much on my mind to care who sat on what throne away down south. And for all Gormant's rage, no one in the village gave the matter much thought. But I had bargained better than I knew for my lady. Now I had the greatest warrior in the island sworn to be her protector. So his threats at the beginning hadn't been an idle boast!

"And may I know the name of the lady I am to wed?" Owain asked, after watching with a smile while I swallowed his news. Something rueful in his tone made me imagine he was thinking that his new north-country bride might make him a laughingstock at that fine southern court.

"My lady's name is Elen, and she has a lineage any lord might be proud of!" I said indignantly. "She is the daughter of Cawdor and Igrayne of Cornwall, who was the daughter of—"

Just then the door lifted and Cei called anxiously, "Luned, are you there, girl?" Owen moved back into the shadows, so that Cei wouldn't see his free hands, but not before I saw the look of blank amazement on his face.

"I'm coming." I gathered my skirts and went up the rough stairs.

"You were a time! What were you doing with him?" Cei leered as he let the door back down, but he was truly curious. "Should I be jealous?"

"I only wanted to know the truth of his quarrel with Gormant," I said, shaking out my skirts.

"And did he tell you? He wouldn't say a word to Siawn."

"He told me. But Elen will want me now—I will explain everything later."

12

ONCE THEY HAD THEIR PRISONER LOCKED UP, no one but Siawn was in much of a hurry to haul him out again and kill him, so it was not hard to insist that we wait until Gormant was decently in the ground before beginning executions. A few of the men went off to the monastery to bring back a priest to do whatever could be done for Gormant's soul. They couldn't be back much before nightfall, so that gave me time to tell Elen what I'd done. She was hardly pleased with the idea of another marriage so soon, but she was wise enough to see it as the best of her choices. And it was brave of her, for men were the things she feared most on earth.

It gave me time to find Cei too and tell him what I needed him to do.

When Father Bedwin arrived at last, we went into the hall with him to pray for Gormant's rest. And I even found myself hoping there might be some peace for Gormant, somewhere he didn't have to throw his heart away to a woman who wanted none of it, and his wits down an ale cask after that. *And peace for the rest of us too, please,* I whispered to any saint who might be listening.

I caught Cei's eye and we slipped out quietly together. While I stayed hidden by the tower wall, Cei went around to the cell to tell Alun that he was there to watch the prisoner. Alun was glad enough for an excuse to go and join the drinking, which, he said, was a better tribute to Gormant's soul than a priest's Latin. I'd knelt to heave the trapdoor open when Cei stopped me with a hand over mine.

"First you keep your promise," he said firmly.

I'd known all along that I'd never be able to carry out my plan without the help of one of Gormant's warriors. And of course it had been Cei that I'd chosen. He was village folk, one of us, and a friend from the days when we'd been children together.

Cei had listened soberly while I explained what I needed. "Risky," he'd said at last, thoughtfully. "And how do you know you can trust this man? He's a stranger here."

And the last time we'd invited a stranger to stay, it hadn't worked out well—he didn't need to remind me. "Would you rather see Siawn our lord then?" I demanded.

"Well, there's that." Cei nodded, frowning, and rubbed at the back of his neck. "All right, then, Luned. I'll help you—for a price."

"A price?" A touch of bitter disappointment made my voice sharp. I hadn't expected Cei to demand—what? land, gold?—in exchange for helping Elen. For helping me. "What price?"

"That you give me my answer before the night's out."

"That old joke?" Suddenly I was angry with him. "Cei, if you think I've time to spare on fooling now—"

"No joke!" To my surprise, Cei was just as angry as I was. "I'll see you tonight, Luned. But before I'll help you, you'll answer me, one way or the other."

And he'd walked off, leaving me stranded somewhere between anger and bewilderment. Just like a man, to hare off after something inconsequential when there were important matters at hand.

But now Cei leaned on the wooden handle of the trapdoor. I knew I'd never pull it up against his weight.

"I've done all the waiting you asked for, girl," he said. "But I want an answer now."

I stared at him. I was almost embarrassed to think it, but he looked as serious as if he weren't playing me for a fool.

"You can't mean it," I told him. "I'm past marrying age. And I've never been—" *Beautiful,* I was going to say, but my tongue got stuck on the word.

"And do I look like some half-grown boy, to want a girl to marry me?" Cei demanded. "What kind of fool do you think I am, not to mean what I say?"

I gaped at him. "But—Gwenllian," I said weakly.

Gwenllian had been Cei's wife and my friend since girlhood. I'd helped sew her wedding dress. She had been sweet and mild and lovely. I was nothing at all like her—a sharp-tongued scold, a woman too busy managing a house and a village and caring for my lady to ever think of marrying.

Cei nodded. His hand pressed down hard on mine. "I loved Gwenllian well. And she's dead these six years, rest her soul. And I know what I want now."

I was as shaken as if he'd suddenly sprouted wings, or summoned a demon to plead his case. He truly wanted me?

He'd never been handsome, Cei—nor was he now, with his thick black eyebrows pulled down in a scowl, the skin of his face and hands and arms marred with the sparks and soot of the forge. But the night was falling between us, softening the blunt lines of his face, and all I could think of was the strength in the hand that held the trapdoor down.

Cei was the strongest man in the village. He could easily sling a full-grown sheep over his shoulders, or beat an iron bar flat as if it were soft as bread dough. But never once, even when we were children, had I seen Cei use that strength to push someone weaker aside.

"Then yes," I told him. "Yes, I will." Cei sat back in surprise, freeing my hand, and I heaved the trapdoor open, peering down into the gloom. "My lord Owain, are you there? Hurry!"

"Where else?" Owain demanded, climbing the steps. He glanced sharply at Cei, but we had no time for introductions.

"Come with me now, hurry, before anyone sees. Cei . . ." I turned to him, and my tongue tripped strangely on emptiness. Twice in one day these two men had struck me dumb. I wasn't at all used to not knowing what to say.

Cei settled things for me by taking a step forward, putting a hand on either side of my face, and kissing me soundly. He was taller than I was. The back of my neck cramped and I could hardly breathe. I was heartily sorry when he let me go.

"Go and get him married then," Cei said, with a nod for Owain. "I'll be waiting here."

I still couldn't find words enough to tell him good-bye. "Your husband?" Owain asked, a little puzzled, as I hurried him away.

"Oh yes," I answered, dizzy and almost drunk with happiness.

By the time we reached my mother's house, I'd become alive again to the peril of what we were doing. Everyone was in Gormant's hall praying, so the hut was a dark, deserted circle, with the banked fire glowing dimly in the center. "Take off your clothes," I commanded. Owain choked, so I went on, flustered. "Well, you can't be married in those, can you? They're covered with mud. Here." I thrust an armful of cloth at him. Not Gormant's best, for Bronwen had taken those to lay him out in, but at least a clean plain linen tunic and good wool trousers. "There's water to wash in there. I'll turn my back, if you're modest."

Before I turned, he caught at my arm. "Did I hear you right before? Is your lady the daughter of Igrayne of Cornwall?"

"She is," I said proudly. We all knew that Igrayne's lineage went back to the ancient kings.

"But then she is—" He broke off as we heard voices outside. They passed by, but I waved my hands at him to hurry, hurry, no more words. You could have fit two of him into Gormant's tunic, but it didn't look too bad with a belt to pull it in at the waist. He'd just finished scrubbing the mud off his face and hair before there were voices at the door, and Elen and Father Bedwin came together into the room.

Elen was frightened by her first sight of Owain, and she looked to me for reassurance before she ventured a few steps closer. She couldn't manage words, but Owain took her faint nod as introduction enough. He told her his name and his parentage, soberly but somehow distracted, and suddenly he lifted a hand to touch a strand of hair that hung by her face. "I never thought a northern woman would be so fair," he said softly, almost to himself. But Elen flinched as his fingers brushed her cheek and only barely stopped herself from stepping away. He snatched his hand back as if her hair had stung.

With his hair still wet from washing and his tunic open at the throat, it seemed a shame to me that such a man should be locked into chaste love with one woman, and into marriage with another who shuddered at his touch. But there was nothing to be done for it now.

To Father Bedwin it seemed a strange meeting of lovers, but we convinced him at last that they both meant to wed. I was in an agony of fretfulness that we might be discovered before it was done. The priest seemed to catch some of my impatience, for I've never seen a quicker wedding. Father Bedwin had barely bidden them rise from their knees when Siawn threw aside the deerskin flap over the door.

He stopped and stood panting, as though a wall had risen up and knocked him breathless. His drawn sword hovered in the air; his face was an angry red. Behind him were Alun and Dafydd and others of Gormant's men. I could hear Bronwen wailing. Owain's hand moved to his hip and groped there for an instant, and I cursed myself up and down for a fool, idiot, lack-wit, to find the man clean clothes and never think of his sword. We would lose everything now, and it would be my fault, my shame forever.

It was Elen who saved us. Before Siawn could lift his sword, she stepped in front of Owain, and I'm glad to say the pendragon had enough sense not to push her aside. I could have shouted with joy, I was so proud of her, of how she stood, slim and slight as a girl, her chin up, protecting her new husband.

It stopped Siawn short. "What's this?" he demanded, his tongue thick, looking from Elen to Owain. Owain, his face full of scorn, was as silent as his wife, as if it were beneath him to answer. For an instant's exasperation I thought they made a proper pair, the two of them. There was no hope for Elen, but someone should have told this pendragon that words are weapons too.

"This is a wedding," I announced. "Father Bedwin has just this moment married them."

I pitched my voice loud enough to be heard by the people I could see behind Siawn, crowding outside the door. Every tongue took up the word, and Siawn had to bellow to make himself heard. "If she's married *that*, she's a traitor, and no true wife! Our lord's murderer!"

"There was no murder!" I shouted it, as loud as Siawn, and stepped forward to keep his eyes on me, away from my lady and her new husband. "It was an honest quarrel, and Gormant struck first!"

"And who told you so? *Him?*" Siawn spat in Owain's direction.

"His word's as good as yours!" I declared. "You weren't there, none of you were!" I dared not take my eyes off Siawn, for that would look like weakness. But I could hear, and there was only silence from the people in the doorway, and a few confused murmurs.

Siawn heard it too, for I saw him give a quick, uneasy glance behind him, just as Owain pushed Elen gently to one side. There was a long, slim dagger in Owain's hand. Where on earth had it come from?

Then Siawn shifted his grip on the hilt of his sword, and I suddenly thought he might well kill me on his way to Owain. "Gormant was drunk; he was likely to quarrel with the first man he met!" I said loudly, desperately. But my words were proving too thin a shield.

Then Father Bedwin, bless him, added his weight. "There will be no bloodshed here!" he broke in, and stepped in front of Siawn. His head barely came up to Siawn's shoulder, but he looked as stern as God himself. "This is consecrated ground. A sacrament has just been performed here. Put away your sword!"

Siawn wasn't quite ready to kill a priest. He fell back a pace, looking around at the people nearby. "Will you believe her? She's a traitor and a liar! She stole this man out of prison, with that bastard traitor Cei, one of my own men—"

"Cei obeyed his *lady's* will!" I shouted. "Elen is lady here, and he only took her orders. Where is he?"

I didn't know I'd won, for I didn't understand the sudden silence. Siawn's mouth opened, but it was as if fear and anger fought in his throat and left him no words. "Where is he?" I repeated. Looking about for an answer, I saw the room full of people frozen in a strange stillness. Even Owain, his knife in his hand, was waiting to hear.

Then Dafydd turned to face me. He was the oldest of Gormant's warriors, his face scarred with all the battles of his long life. He was still limping from his encounter with Owain that morning. And, strangely, he looked at me in something like honest grief. "We found Cei by the cell, and the prisoner gone. It was like Siawn went mad." Dafydd stood barely a foot from me, but his voice was far away. "Through the heart. Cei never even touched his sword."

For the first time I saw that Siawn's sword was streaked with red; blood had run down the channels and dripped over the hilt and his fist.

I felt as if someone had hit me, hard enough to break ribs and drive the sharp pieces of bone through my heart. Cei could not be dead. He'd said he would be waiting. Cei never broke his word.

A glowing chunk of charcoal broke loose from a log in the hearth. It fell with a soft thump, muffled by ashes. In the quiet of that room, it sounded like a hammer on an anvil.

But the silence this time wasn't waiting. It was angry.

Cei was village folk, one of us. To Gormant's warriors as well, he was one of their own. And Siawn had killed him without an accusation, without a trial, without even giving him the chance to draw a weapon.

Siawn looked around for support, and found none. The village people pressed in closer to the door. Even Alun, who was Gormant's kin, frowned as he glanced at the faces of the people in the doorway, and shook his head when Siawn's eyes met his.

Dafydd turned to stand by my side, with a hand on his sword. "You aren't lord here," he said to Siawn.

The threat behind the silence built and grew until Siawn turned away, blundering past people into the night.

They let him go. For a year or so he stayed away, until he took to stealing stock and robbing travelers. Then Owain led a band to hunt him down, and he died on the hillside with someone's arrow in his throat, and they left him there for the scavengers.

But that came later. For now, Elen came to kneel beside me as my knees folded and I sank to the ground. She held me tightly as I dragged in one painful breath and let it out in a cry that felt like it would never end.

So my lady's second wedding was a bitter celebration for me, even more so than for her. But even while I grieved for Cei, I still thought my bargain with Owain had been well made. He stayed with us some months, and people came to—well, not *like* him; he was not friendly enough for that, slow to speak or smile, and in his quiet way much more of a lord than Gormant, for all his bluster, had ever been. But they did come to trust him. And when they found out who he really was, they were simply relieved that we were not all bound to suffer a blood feud or pay compensation all our lives for imprisoning Arthur the Conqueror's pendragon. No one was inclined to make a fuss over accepting him as our new lord.

Owain made a better lord than any of us could have hoped. But as a husband for Elen—well, I decided much later that it would have been better for my lady if I'd maneuvered to marry her to Dafydd or even Father Bedwin—the pope may not like his priests to marry, but Rome's far away and most of the saints never minded. Or if Owain had not turned out to be Owain after all, but a common everyday highway thief.

Well, how was I to know she would fall in love with him?

I thought I knew Elen and that all men were the same to her—something to be avoided if she could, endured if she could not. But I should have known, remembering how Elen had stepped before Siawn's sword to protect her new husband, that Owain was different to her.

Just what it was that made him different I can't say. He was southern-tongued, of course, courtly mannered, and sweetly handsome, although I never saw Elen look him in the face, so how she knew if he was handsome or not is a mystery. Maybe it was gratitude to begin with, for he gave her a great gift—the gift of her kin. Elen was as surprised as I was when he told her that his lord, Arthur, was Igrayne of Cornwall's son. Few of us this far north had ever heard the truth of Arthur's parentage. So Owain brought her a brother as a marriage gift. Maybe that began it, her silent adoration of him.

Or maybe it was a curse from Gormant's ghost, that she should love someone as hopelessly as he had loved her.

Owain always treated Elen with the same gentle, distant courtesy. Since their wedding he never touched so much as a strand of her hair. And he never once looked at her carefully enough to see what he had caused.

I began to worry a month or two after their marriage, but I thought that he would soon be gone back south, and that would end things. When he did depart, leaving Dafydd in charge, Elen was quieter than ever. I prayed to any available saint to take Gormant's curse away. And they did answer, as it happened, although I thought at first they had misheard my prayer.

13

WAIN CAME BACK after an absence of some years, bringing a boy with him. Six or seven years old, as fair as Elen herself, he stood in the hall much as Elen had done so long ago: the same stillness, the same silent fright. Elen looked amazed at Owain, but without a word she went quickly to the boy as I had once done to her, to comfort and protect.

The boy's name was Gwydre, and he was the son of Arthur and his once-wife, Elen's sister Morgan. Owain told Elen that the boy was Arthur's heir, and would be king someday.

There were reasons Owain gave why he wanted the child brought up as his son and Elen's, but they were all to do with southern politics, and I didn't pay much attention. I was only concerned with Elen, and it was obvious from the start that she thought of the boy as her own. But Owain insisted that she take him elsewhere to be raised, since everyone at home knew she'd never borne a child. He found her a nunnery to go to, with a monastery close by. My mother had died the winter before, and after Cei's death I had no heart for marrying anyone else. So I went with Elen and her new son.

The sisters all made a pet of Gwydre, Elen adored him, and I was fond of him myself. He was in fair danger of being spoiled, until he was sent to the monks' school and learned to read and write and sing Latin in a tuneless voice. There was a workshop where the brothers made candlesticks and patens and goblets for the mass, and it was there Gwydre was happiest, hunched over squinting with his weak blue eyes at some intricate glistening bit of work, humming bad Latin between his teeth.

Elen was content in the nunnery, while she had Gwydre to watch over and no men except monks to trouble her. I managed the kitchens and the storerooms, and every time I prayed, I gave thanks that my lady had peace at last.

Well, I never claimed to be wise.

Owain had been in the habit of coming two or three times a year, to see how Gwydre was growing, and if he was shaping up into a fine king. Which was pure foolishness, and I or anyone could have told him so. The boy was shaping up into a fine silversmith, but he'd never make a king. Like most men, however, Owain was blind and deaf to what he didn't want to see or hear. He even did his best to teach the boy swordcraft, though the abbot disapproved. Elen and I lived in terror that Gwydre would slice his own fingers off or crack someone's skull by mistake.

When Gwydre was sixteen, Owain came for what he said was the last time. He greeted his wife courteously, stayed the night, and left for the south the next morning, taking Gwydre with him.

The boy didn't want to go, but between the monks' teaching and Elen's example, he'd thoroughly drunk in the idea that life was full of hardships you endured without complaint. Elen didn't say a word of protest. After they had ridden away she spoke to me where we stood together at the gate, watching.

"He will never come back this time," she said, so quietly you could hardly hear the heartbreak in her voice.

Without Gwydre or the hope of seeing Owain, Elen began to

drift away. She didn't mean to—I know she'd never have meant to leave me behind. But as a year went by, she began to forget things. Forgot to eat, forgot to sleep at night. I would find her in the morning, sitting by a southern window, dozing with her face against the stones. The sisters thought she was very holy. But I was afraid she would forget to breathe one day if something wasn't done.

You would think poor Cei had cured me of managing other people. But if Elen died, of a broken heart or sheer empty-headedness, I would have no one left to take care of. And that idea frightened me so badly that I bargained with a traveling merchant to take me as far south as Arthur's court.

CAMELOT WAS A JUMBLE OF BUILDINGS AND STREETS clustered on a flat-topped hill, sheltered inside a wall that would have made any raiding party think twice. Everything looked new-built: no gaps in the walls, no roofless houses or empty buildings. My trader took me to the marketplace, where he set up his stall and pointed me toward the court on the top of the hill.

Before I got there, I ducked into an alley between a shepherd's and a smithy, and tried to make myself look worthy of a visit with the king's pendragon. I dug my shoes out of my bundle and hid my muddy feet inside them, and combed my hair with my fingers. Dipping a corner of my cloak into the sheeps' water trough, I used it to wash my face and hands. Since the shepherd came out to stare at me, I smiled at him, straightened my dress, and started up the hill.

I expected an argument when I told the gatekeeper I wanted to see Owain Pendragon, since I hardly looked the part of a royal lady's messenger. But he only shrugged and led me inside with the air of a man who'd seen far stranger sights than me. Lord Owain was in the practice yard, he told me, and found a skinny, scraggly-haired servant boy to show me the way.

The practice yard was a trampled square beside the great

hall, more mud than grass, with archers at one end and sword and spearmen at the other, all hammering away at each other and making a clamor of steel and wood. The boy pointed Owain out for me, and went to tell him I was there. I didn't want to have my head lopped off by an ill-aimed blow just as I was at the end of my errand, so I waited across the yard as the boy went twisting and winding like an eel among the pairs of struggling men.

Idly, I watched the two closest to me, one with a sword and shield, the other with a spear. They wore no helmets, and the swordsman's face teased at my memory with a faint resemblance I couldn't place. He was young, lithe, dark-haired, pale-skinned. It wasn't the eyes, dark and intent, or the straight brows pulled down over them in a scowl. Something about the mouth? He'd spared me a glance when I first arrived, not curious, simply noting my presence. But when the servant boy called Owain's name loudly and pointed at me, the swordsman looked up quickly to stare. His opponent deftly hooked a foot behind his ankle and yanked him off balance. He went down flat on his back, and the other lunged and stopped with his spear an inch from his throat, laughing at him.

The dark man knocked the spear away and scrambled to his feet, angry. But by that time Owain was at my side, and I didn't get to see if it turned into a full-blown fight. "Luned, is it you? What are you doing here?" He didn't give me a chance to answer before he glanced over at the two men I'd been watching and shouted angrily, "Medraud, Gareth, put on your helmets! Arthur won't thank me for a pair of cracked skulls."

"I've finished," the swordsman said, a bit sullenly, coming over to us. "Who's your visitor?"

"A messenger," Owain said shortly. "Come inside, Luned, I'll hear you there." I followed him, leaving the other man standing and looking after us, thoughtful.

"Who was that?" I asked as Owain led me into the hall—huge; Gormant's hall would have fit into it six times over with room to spare.

"No one for you to be concerned with," Owain answered shortly. We went to his chambers, where he threw his blunt practice sword down onto the pile of bed furs and waved me to a seat on a chest. "Now, what is it? Is something wrong with Elen?"

The exact opening I wanted. "Very wrong," I said quickly. "So I've come to ask something of you."

"Is she sick? Does she need a doctor?" He sat down on another chest, concerned. "One of the priests here knows medicine. I'll send him north with you."

"He can't help her."

"It's that bad?" He was worried, but not soul-stricken. If Elen was indeed ill, if she died, he would grieve a bit, as though for a distant relative, and go on without truly mourning. I was reminded of the time I sat across from him in the darkness of the root cellar and bargained for his life and my lady's safety. Now her peace was in the bargain again, but this time I had nothing much to trade with.

I tried, nonetheless. "It's bad enough. But she doesn't need a doctor or a priest. She needs you. I came to ask you to come and see her."

Owain looked startled. "To see her? Why?"

Exasperation overcame my resolution for patience and calm. "Because she loves you, you fool! She always has. She's pining for you, and if she doesn't see you, I think she'll go mad. Or die."

You'd think I'd hit him over the head with a club. He sat gaping at me, and then blinked and swallowed and said, "She loves me? But she's never said three words to me—"

"That's not stopping her." I scowled at him. Idiot, to wreck my lady's peace and not even notice he was doing it. "I don't say you have to stay long, or go often. Once a year, twice, as you did when Gwydre was there. You don't even have to say you love her. Just see her. That's all she needs. It isn't that much to ask."

"It's more than I'd planned on giving." He looked embarrassed, and rubbed at the back of his neck with his hand. "Luned, you don't know what you're asking."

"I'm asking you to see your wife," I said tartly. "It isn't that hard."

"It's harder than you know." He stood up abruptly and began to pace, stopping every two or three steps to turn around. His steps were as neat and light and cat-precise as ever. "This wasn't in our bargain, Luned. That I would love her, or she would love me—"

"Neither was a son," I pointed out. "But Elen raised him for you, and never complained. You owe her for that."

"Maybe I do." He stopped pacing. "But you know I have another love, Luned. I told you so from the first."

"I'm not asking you to love Elen. Just see her. Once a year . . ."

He was wavering a bit. There was a gentleness in him, touched with pity, for Elen—he would never love her, but he didn't want her to suffer. "What did you mean, she'll die if I don't see her?"

"You know she isn't like other women. She's fey, strange—not mad, but she's not *here,* not like we are. The nuns say she hears voices." I struggled to explain my lady to this man who'd married her but didn't love her, didn't know her, barely saw her. "She isn't a child, though she seems like one. She feels things, not like we do, where the feeling is a wind and we're the rock it breaks on, and we aren't touched, aren't changed. The wind takes her, she can't withstand it. When she's frightened, she's terrified. And when she loves . . ."

Owain stood listening, perfectly still.

"You saved her once, and I saved you," I begged. "Save her again. She needs something else to love, now Gwydre's gone."

It took a bit more coaxing than that, but he did finally come north with me. Thinking of the joy it would give Elen to see him, I didn't mind that he was grim and silent most of the journey. At the sight of him, Elen broke into a smile that might have convinced even her blind husband of her love for him. He stayed for a week, and Elen came out of her moods enough to eat, and answer when she was spoken to, and take an interest in what was around her.

I had many eager audiences myself, for a time, as all the servants and even the sisters demanded to know everything I had seen and heard and tasted and touched on my visit to Arthur's court. I told it all—how I had seen the king himself, who was tall and almost as fair as Elen, with a smile that was warm as a fire in midwinter. How I had seen the queen too, lovely and proud. I didn't say that one glance at her braids, yellow as gorse flowers, had made me remember how Owain had touched Elen's hair in astonishment the first time he'd seen her, and made me sure who his mysterious married lover was.

But all the women were satisfied to hear of the size of the hall, how it was crowded with Arthur's warriors and craftsmen and farmers and herdsmen, the rich and colorful clothes, the food I tasted, the golden plates and silver goblets filled with sweet southern wine at the high table. If I invented a few details for them, what harm? None of them were ever likely to see for themselves.

Owain said he would come again before the year was out. Elen tells me, as she waits for him, of all the things he talked about during his stay—battles and truces and alliances. Well, southern kingdoms and kings are none of my concern, or they never would have been, if Gormant hadn't pointed his finger at me in that dark tower room so many years ago, when Elen and I were both no more than girls.

If Gormant hadn't pointed his finger at me, I would never have sat in a root cellar and struck a bargain with the high king's pendragon. I'd never have seen Arthur's court, or helped to raise a king's heir. Perhaps I would have married Cei earlier, the first time he'd asked me; perhaps we would have had children together. And I never would have had Elen for my little sister, almost my child, someone to take care of all these years.

Medraud

14

MY FATHER IS DYING.

He lies with his head in my lap, and his face is so quiet, so drained of blood, that I can see every faint line in the skin. He may be dead already. A few minutes ago I held my fingers over his lips and thought I could feel his breath against them. But my hands are frozen stiff, and it is hard to feel anything. The cold weighs down on me, heavy as a shirt of woven mail. Only my blood, against my side, is warm.

When I was younger my mother would tell me stories as we sat before the kitchen fire, the only warm place in that whole sea-damp, wind-battered, Cornish wreck of a castle. Stories about the ancient people who built the stone circles and dug caves in the hillside. Of Gwyn ap Nudd and his host of shining warriors who never raised a sword, but terrified their enemies by the light of their faces. And over and over, because I asked for it so often, the story of Lleu and Dylan. The twin brothers, light and dark, lucky and unlucky, living and dead.

The story, like everything else, is Lleu's—how cleverly he evaded his mother's curse that he should have no name, or weapon, or wife. But it was Dylan who stayed in my mind, trespassing even into my dreams: the dark brother who wandered the shore, crying for love of the sea. On the edge of the surf, in the white foam, in the place that is neither land nor water, he was killed by his uncle's spear and his blood flowed into the waves.

I WAS SEVEN YEARS OLD the first time I saw my father. My brother Gwydre and I had just climbed the steep, rocky path that led up the cliffs from the beach. We were headed toward the kitchen to warm our feet and dry our shoes by the fire.

But I stopped in the doorway to the hall, staring. My mother was there, and a man I didn't know. Neither one noticed us. I pressed myself against the wall, listening, and gestured to Gwydre to do the same. If I had been older I might have seen that the man resembled my brother—the same light hair, the same fair skin—although Gwydre's eyes were blue and this man's dark brown. As it was, I just saw a tall, bearded stranger, still wearing the long fur-lined cloak and the tall boots he had put on for riding.

"They are all I have." My mother was angry. I could easily see the tension in her body and hear it in her low, quick voice, like the tension that pulls through the wood of a strung bow. "You cannot take them from me."

"They are mine as well as yours." The man's voice was carefully low, as though he were trying not to shout. "I have left them with you seven years, Morgan. They are more than old enough for fosterage."

"Let your new wife give you sons."

"She cannot."

My mother smiled maliciously. "Is it my fault you were fool enough to take a barren woman?"

"Enough!" The word was a command. "I am not here to argue with you, Morgan. They are my sons, and must be brought up as my heirs."

She turned on him. "You threw me off, and you exiled me here—"

"You chose to come here, and you chose to end our marriage—"

"And now you will take my sons from me as well. Is there nothing you will leave me?"

Take us? He would take us—where? Why? I looked over at Gwydre, saw his eyes wide with shock like my own. Suddenly he turned and ran, away from the hall, back down toward the path that led to the water. There were caves and hollows in the rocks at the base of the cliffs, and Gwydre knew them all. He could hide there for hours and never be found. He'd done it before.

But I didn't follow him. I pressed myself close against the wall, as if I could melt into it and never been seen. If this were a threat—and it seemed to be so—I needed, not to run, but to watch and listen. I needed to know more.

Neither my mother nor the stranger had noticed the sound of Gwydre's feet on the ground. "Morgan, have sense!" The man—my *father*?—raked a hand through his hair, and a gold ring on his thumb caught the light. "You could live anywhere in my realm, if you wanted, and as my sister, even at Camelot. And the only reason I have not asked you there is that I know you would not accept!" He let out a sharp and angry breath. "And I did not cast you off. You asked for a divorce, in the old manner. I am the one who has a right to be angry—you didn't even tell me you were carrying my sons!"

"I didn't know, then—and how do you know they are yours?" She threw the words at him, a challenge, but his face showed only impatience in response.

"Morgan, the fair one is my own image, I have been told. Stop this, will you? I need an heir. Do you want what happened to this land when Uther died to happen again?" She turned abruptly away without answering. He tried coaxing her, softening his voice. "Is it so hard, Morgan, that one of your sons should grow up to be king?"

She had her back to him, so I was the only one who could see the look of slow calculation that slid over her face. She turned to face him, so quickly her skirt swirled around her legs. "Very well. Take one of them. But not both—Arthur, you can't take both of them from me. You wouldn't be so cruel, you wouldn't leave me so alone." The slanting sunlight threw shadows under her eyebrows, making her eyes look wide and piteous. Arthur nodded.

"I never wished to cause you pain, Morgan. I will take the oldest boy as my heir. Which one . . . ?"

I was ready to turn and run, following Gwydre, when my mother spoke. "Gwydre," she answered him. "Gwydre, the fair one. He is the oldest."

I think I must have made some sound, because they both turned toward me in surprise. My mother held out her hand. "Medraud! Come and meet your father." I expected a slap for having been caught listening, but she only put her arm around my shoulders and drew me forward. Her fingers tightened on my upper arm until the ache went down to the bone and I understood the warning: I was not to tell my father the truth about which of his sons had been born first.

"This is Medraud, Arthur."

Arthur was tall. He crouched down to bring his head on a level with mine. "I am glad to know you, at last," he said formally, and offered a tentative smile, which I did not return. I only pressed closer against my mother, trying to ease the pressure of her fingers on my arm, and stared at him.

He looked kind, but I did not trust him. He had appeared from nowhere, like a ghost or a spirit, and my mother had lied to keep me from him. My mother had lied to keep me from my father, but she'd given my brother away with barely a qualm.

Growing up beside the sea, you quickly learn that water can never be trusted. The quiet ocean can turn overnight into a howling beast, clawing at the land, trying to drown you in your bed. Water that looks placid and smooth can hide currents that will swallow you alive, or sharp rocks that will cripple a boat or kill a swimmer. You learn to watch the wind, the tides. You learn never to believe the promise of a sunlit day. You learn to be aware, always, of what a shift in the wind might bring. Of what lies hidden beneath the surface.

So I watched my father carefully, trying to uncover the truth underneath his smile. The familiar space of the hall seemed somehow too big; I was lost, adrift. Where was the greatest danger here? With this stranger, my father, who had suddenly appeared to tear our family apart? Or with my mother, who might give me away as easily as she'd given up my brother?

The bruises were still on my arm three days later, as I stood with my mother in the doorway, watching my brother and father ride away. It had not taken Gwydre long, after all, to get over his fear of our father. Before a full day had passed he was talking to Arthur as if he'd always known him, proudly showing him the best of his treasures: the shells and wave-worn stones, the white gull's feathers he collected. Arthur would listen seriously, his eyes bright with interest, while I stood silently outside the circle of their talk, watching. I couldn't find the words to warn my brother not to trust so quickly.

At the last, Gwydre had cried and clung to our mother, but Arthur had been patient with him, and finally coaxed him away. I didn't cry, any more than our mother did. Sunlight made the quiet sea shine smooth as glass. My father's hair, when he knelt to embrace me, glowed warm as fire. I stood stiff within his arms, waiting for him to let me go.

We watched until they were out of sight, Arthur on his tall horse, Gwydre on a stocky pony beside him. Then my mother knelt and put her arm around me, pulling me tight against her.

"You are all I have now," she said.

She never spoke again of Gwydre after that day. It was as if I never had a brother, and the shells and stones and pieces of sea-sculpted wood scattered through my room had been left there by the tide.

15

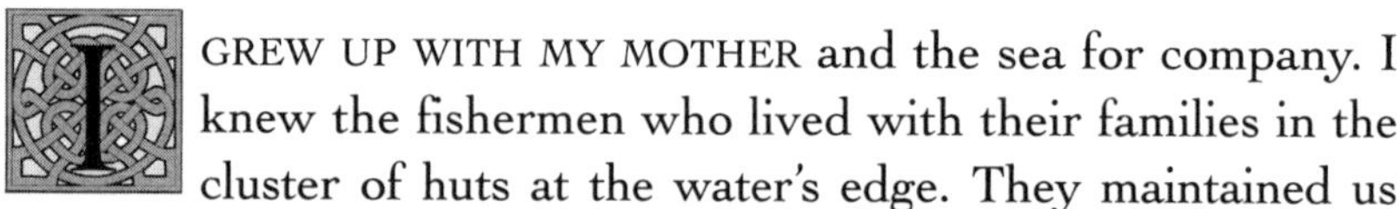

I GREW UP WITH MY MOTHER and the sea for company. I knew the fishermen who lived with their families in the cluster of huts at the water's edge. They maintained us with their tribute of salted fish and dark, sour beer. But I didn't know them well. They were proud of my mother, their lady, proud that she had once been high queen, prouder that she was of the blood of my grandmother, who was of the blood of the ancient kings. They relied on her knowledge of herbs and old cures and fortune-telling, and some came to her in secret to get charms for their boats and wards against sickness. But most of them thought she was a little mad, or a witch, and so they kept their distance from both of us.

On good days my mother would sing, and laugh, or take off her shoes and run through the surf like a girl. I would curl up by the kitchen fire with my head in her lap, and she would tell me stories.

"Do you know how Bran avenged his sister's shame?" she asked one evening. I'd heard the story before, but I shook my head. Her voice, when it was telling stories, was calm, her hands gentle, her fingers combing softly through my hair. I would have listened happily to the same tale a hundred times over.

"Bran, son of Llyr, had a sister, the loveliest maiden in the island," she began. The wind howled outside and twigs snapped in the heat of the fire. The salt in the driftwood made little lines of purple and blue dance along the edges of the flames.

The story at an end, with Bran dead of a poisoned wound and his sister Branwen of a broken heart, my mother sat quietly for a while. I lay still, warm and content. "Enough, Medraud! Leave me be!" she said abruptly, pushing me from her. Unprepared, I nearly tumbled into the fire. My mother wrapped her arms around her knees, staring into the flames, looking angry and unhappy all at once.

I'd crawled back a few feet, preparing to slip away, when she spoke. "Family, Medraud. It's the most important thing, do you understand that?" I nodded. Nothing made her angrier than for me to try and leave while she was speaking. I sat down at a little distance from her.

"Bran threw his kingdom into war to avenge his sister," my mother told me. "There's no honor if you don't defend your own family. That's what your father never understood."

Her dark hair drifted a little in the warm air from the fire. "Coward," she said softly. "Brave enough on the battlefield, but too weak to avenge his own mother. Traitor. Son of a murderer."

"Why did you give Gwydre to him then?" I asked. I was still half asleep, or I would never have been so reckless. She hit me hard enough to cut the inside of my cheek against my teeth and make it painful to chew my food for days.

I should have known better than to mention Gwydre to her. And after that one time, I never did again. At night, alone and awake in my tower room, I would sometimes whisper my brother's name. In the daylight I never looked for him; I knew he was gone. But in the dark I couldn't help thinking that he might be hidden somewhere nearby. That this time he might actually answer me.

He never did. And there were times I wondered if I'd really had a twin. I thought I remembered him, sitting cross-legged on the floor, arranging his seashore treasures in endless patterns. It used to make me mad with restlessness to watch him, setting stones here, shells there, or lining them up in rows. He could sit without moving for hours.

He would come outdoors, though, whenever I asked. We'd explore the sea caves or run along the shore. With driftwood swords we practiced fighting on the beach, rescuing our stony kingdom from sea raiders and Saxon armies.

But maybe I couldn't even trust my own memories. Maybe I'd dreamed him, dreamed the day our father had come to take him. Or maybe I'd once had a brother, but he had died in the fever that had sickened us both when we were very young. Gwydre's illness had been much worse than mine, and he had taken longer to recover. Maybe he never had. Maybe all those years afterward my companion had been a spirit, gone back now to his place in the shadow world. Maybe ghosts could be lonely too.

AS I GREW OLDER, there were things my mother insisted I learn. She found men to teach me swordcraft and horsemanship and strategy, wandering soldiers who came our way looking for a lord to serve. If she approved of them she'd ask them to stay for a time. I can hardly remember any of their names, but I loved what they had to teach me—the shock of metal on metal, the dull clang of a well-parried blow.

It was all very clear, straightforward. If you parried a blow well, you were safe; if not, you were knocked sprawling, with bruises the next day to show for it. Practice swords might be blunt, but they were all the heavier for the weight of the extra metal.

There's never any confusion when you have a sword in your hand. You either hit someone or are hit yourself, and all that matters is the moment of the blow. Swordcraft was simple. It was safety.

And I learned it quickly. My teachers praised me, but I didn't need their words to know that I was getting better. It wasn't just that fewer strokes got through my defenses, or that I soon started to land blows on my teachers instead of the other way around. It was the comfort of the hilt in my hand, the way the sword seemed to know where it should be before my mind could tell it.

My mother paid a blacksmith from a nearby village to make me my first sword. It was a plain thing, even ugly; the man had no skill for decoration, and we had no gold to spare, no jewels or glass to beautify it.

I didn't care. The blacksmith may have been no artist, but he knew how to hammer metal straight and true. The hilt felt solid and warm in my hand. The balance was good; I didn't have to strain to hold the blade up. After the weight of the clumsy practice swords, it felt as light as straw. The sharp edge nearly sang as it cut through the air.

My mother paid the warriors who taught me with food and lodging and gold from the dwindling store of coins and rings she kept in the chest in her room. If they expected another kind of payment—and they may have done, for my mother was beautiful, still slim as a girl, with her dark hair always slipping free of its braid to hang loose around her face—then they were disappointed. My mother had small use for men, and an acid tongue, and a knife that never left her belt.

Things were different with another of my teachers. He was a bard, and he taught me the harp, and many of the old stories and songs. His name was Accolon.

He'd arrived one day, the year I was fourteen, and asked for a bard's three nights of lodging. We'd had bards at our court before, but never any that could play the way he could. When he saw how intently I was watching his fingers on the strings, he smiled and offered to teach me.

I don't know what it was about him that made my mother look at him differently than at the warriors who taught me, or even the village fishermen. Maybe it was only that he never seemed surprised or hurt at her sharp tongue, her scalding rage. Nothing she ever said or did seemed to alarm or anger him. And I think that easy calm of his was somehow restful to her.

I came to like his quiet presence by the fire in the evenings. And my mother grew gentler around him, her harsh edges softened, her impatient, restless movements eased. The days she wouldn't speak at all became fewer and farther between.

Most of the warriors who taught me swordcraft thought a slap to set my ears ringing was the best way to correct a mistake. Accolon never even raised his voice. "No one ever got it right the first time," he'd say, smiling, when I'd struck a hash of wrong notes enough to make his harp sound like a cat yowling for a mate. "Hold your hand this way, do you see? And try it again."

It was strange that music should remind me of swordcraft. But the wood of Accolon's harp against my shoulder felt as right as a sword hilt in my hand. And plucking a song carefully, note by note, out of the strings—somehow there was safety in that too. Music had an order, a pattern to it; there was no confusion, no surprises, no danger.

I WAS SIXTEEN, and Accolon had been staying with us for nearly two years, the night sea raiders attacked the fishing village. We were sitting, all three of us, around the fire, listening to Accolon's harp. It wasn't one of the old songs he was playing; it was a strange, uneasy music with no beginning and no end. Accolon said he was trying to make the harp sound like the wind that whined and sighed and whimpered and howled around the crumbling stones of our castle, never still.

Another sound teased its way under the notes of the music to my ear. It bothered me that I couldn't make it out. Leaving Accolon and my mother, I slipped quietly out of the kitchen. I thought I might hear better outdoors.

I could. Shouting, voices raised in anger and panic, sounded faintly above the noise of the waves. I moved to the edge of the cliff and looked over, to the broad stretch of beach where the houses of the fishermen huddled down by the water. The moon was almost full, and there was just enough dim gray light to let me see the black bulk of a ship, perhaps forty feet long, visible against the dark water as it drew near to the shore.

I ran to my room, shouting to my mother and Accolon what was happening. I snatched my sword from its chest. It was long for me, and almost tripped me as I ran, trying to fasten the sword belt around my waist without slowing down.

I was lucky I didn't land on the beach with a broken neck in my headlong rush. Fortunately my feet knew every rock and hollow in the cliff path. In a few minutes I was scrambling across the stony beach toward the dark figures struggling by the water's edge. I drew my sword as I ran.

I never thought of it as being reckless. It was necessary. My mother may not have kept much of a court, but she was the lady here, and I was the closest thing to a warrior she had. And these were our people. They paid us tribute, they bowed their heads in respect when we came near. In return we owed them whatever protection we could give.

There were perhaps fifteen of the raiders. Irish, I could tell by their voices, armed mostly with clubs and knives. A few had swords—stolen, no doubt. The moonlight was bright enough to show their shapes, but nothing of their faces, and it robbed everything of color; all I could see was shades of gray against the black of sea and sky. "Light!" I screamed at the top of my lungs. "We need light!"

One of the shapes turned toward me, but I hesitated. I could see nothing of his face but a glint of bared teeth. Was he a raider, or one of the fisherman? Then the moonlight glanced off the blade he swung at me, a streak of silver in the dark. Easy enough. Now I *knew* he was an enemy.

Before I could think, my arm moved, my blade knocking his aside. The iron rang true, a good sound, familiar. His blade was back again, stabbing at my ribs; I moved to parry, but it had only been a feint. The sword swung up, aiming at my face. I had to jump back. Stones shifted under my feet, and I nearly fell.

Strangely, I felt myself calm. There was no fear, not even any anger toward this stranger whose sword had come within a few inches of spilling my life's blood on the stones. I didn't hate him, I wasn't afraid of him. I was only going to kill him.

I swung for his sword arm, but dropped my blade a few inches as he moved his own to meet it. His sword flew over mine, whistling in the air. I let my stroke continue, dropping down, and my sword cut deep into the muscle of his thigh, just above the knee. The blood looked black. He screamed as he fell, but stopped as the tip of my sword slid into his throat.

The blood this time looked red. Some of the women and girls had brought torches; the warm light slipped across the cold gray stones. Standing for a moment, suddenly hearing my own breathing loud in my ears, I saw one of the girls, no older than I was, swing her torch into the face of the raider who had hold of her arm. He howled and staggered back with his beard aflame. But she didn't see the man behind her, the one who grabbed the torch and wrenched it from her hand before dragging her toward the boat.

My stroke was too early. I swung when I was still running toward them, and the tip of my blade only cut through the rough brown cloth of his sleeve. I'd meant to take his hand off. But he flung the girl away, sending her sprawling over the stones, as he turned to face me.

He only had a club. With one look at my bloody sword, he began to back away.

I didn't go after him. Looking around, I saw two of the raiders seize a woman by her arms, dragging her through the knee-deep water. They heaved her, screaming, over the side of the boat. One of the fishermen charged after her with a roar and was clubbed to his knees. Men were fighting in pairs all over the beach.

It wouldn't work. The raiders were better fighters, better armed. They could pick us off easily, scattered and separate like this.

"Get back!" I shouted, as loud as I could. "Get back to the boats!" The fishing boats were drawn up on the beach between the raiders' ship and the houses of the village. They would do for a line of defense.

I kept shouting until they obeyed me. We stood behind the boats, a ragtag line of fishermen. Except for me, no one was armed with anything better than an axe. The girl I'd saved was beside me, a heavy stone clutched in her hand. The raiders drew back a little. The pause was only a few heartbeats long, but I've never known my heart beat so slowly.

One of the raiders shrugged, and spat, and made a gesture to the rest. They backed away and scrambled into the boat. We stood watching as they heaved at the oars, moving the heavy boat out against the surf. The wailing of the captives they'd managed to seize lingered in the air.

I started to sheathe my sword, but it was still sticky with blood. I looked around for something to clean it with, and at last I wiped it dry on my tunic. But when I put the sword away, my hand, with nothing to hold, began to shake. I clenched it into a fist, but it wouldn't be still.

"Young lord."

I looked up to see Madoc standing before me. Huge, burly, and black-haired, strong enough to pull a net full of fish into a boat single-handed, he was the closest thing they had to a leader in the village. He had one arm around the girl I'd saved, an ax in his other hand. The girl's braid had come undone, the red-brown strands of her hair curling around her face. I thought that I ought to be able to remember her name.

Madoc bent his head to me. "Well done, young lord," he said soberly.

I nodded back. There didn't seem to be anything more to say, so I turned and headed for the cliff path.

My mother was standing quietly near the foot of the cliff, her arms folded across her chest. Accolon was beside her, his usual calm shaken. Bards weren't allowed to touch weapons, but he held a heavy wooden club. My mother's face was unreadable. But she reached out a hand as I drew near them and laid it softly on my arm.

"They took Goewin," Accolon said. He looked sick. "And Meilyr. Cynan's dead—"

"We're lucky they didn't take more," I answered. My own voice sounded strange in my ears, as if I hadn't spoken for days. But it was true. We were lucky the village was still standing, lucky we weren't all dead or bound in the bottom of a raiding boat, on our way to Ireland and slavery.

"Lucky?" Accolon looked down at the club he was holding and dropped it onto the stones. "I thought surely they were going to charge us. We never could have held them off." He looked quizzically at me. "How did you know they wouldn't?"

I hadn't known; I'd only hoped. "They weren't expecting a

fight," I explained. "There would have been more of them, and better armed." They'd thought we were easy prey—one night's effort, a few slaves, a fair profit at little risk. "We would have killed at least a few. They weren't willing to risk it."

Accolon shook his head. "You thought of all that?"

I couldn't understand his bewilderment. Hadn't it been obvious?

To my surprise, my mother reached out to brush my hair back and kissed me gently on the forehead. Almost as if she'd been worried for me—as if she was proud of me. "Come," she said, and turned toward the cliff path.

We climbed in silence. I was thinking of the man I'd killed. In the dark, I'd never seen his face.

Since then, I've heard warriors say that their first kill had sickened them, haunted their dreams. But I only thought how surprisingly easy it was, the softness of flesh to the eager edge of the blade. And how calm. There was no enmity in it, no rage. Just that dance of metal on metal, and its final end.

In the kitchen, Accolon knelt to add wood to the fire. When the flames were bright he settled back on his heels with a sigh. "I need a drink. That was—" He broke off, frowning. "Medraud, what's wrong with your hand?"

I looked down in surprise. There was a deep gash across the back of my left hand, laying open the white knucklebones. I had no idea how it had happened.

Accolon pushed me gently down by the fire and took hold of my hand. Carefully he bent each finger, making sure nothing was broken. It hadn't hurt until he'd called my attention to it. Now I had to grind my teeth together to keep from crying out.

"We'll need some bandages," Accolon said. "Where's—"

My mother came into the room, carrying a roughly carved wooden bowl, full of water, and an old, worn linen tunic. Without a word, she began ripping the cloth into strips. Accolon watched as she cleaned the cut. Her fingers, marked by old scars that showed pink and white against the skin, were gentle. She wrapped the bandages tightly around my hand until no red showed against the white cloth.

She was silent the whole time. Accolon was the one who spoke. "You'll have to take better care of your hands than that," he said, in the closest thing to a reproach I had ever heard from him.

"It's not my sword hand," I said. I flexed my fingers gingerly. They seemed to work.

"You need both hands for the harp," Accolon pointed out.

"He isn't to be a bard." My mother's harsh voice startled us both. All her gentleness seemed gone. Her face might have been carved from stone.

"I know that, Morgan." Accolon picked his harp up from where it lay abandoned on the floor, his hands cradling it tenderly. For the first time I heard protest in his voice as he looked at my mother. "But anyone would think he's going to lead armies, the way you have him train. Is it really—"

"In half a year he'll be seventeen."

"And then what?"

"Then he'll be old enough."

She sat just beyond the edge of the firelight. Her flat voice and her shadowed face made me uneasy. It seemed almost as if she were a priestess of the old religion, and it was my fate she was foretelling.

"Old enough for what?"

"To honor his family."

"Morgan!" Accolon looked both alarmed and exasperated. "He's just a boy! This isn't some story out of the old days. You're not really going to hang that vengeance on him—Morgan, surely—"

"My son is no concern of yours!"

Accolon should have known better than to argue with her when her voice sounded like that. For some reason I didn't want to watch them quarreling. I got quietly to my feet and slipped out of the room. Neither one noticed.

The stone stairs up to my room seemed endless. I hadn't remembered to bring a light, but I didn't need one. Clumsily, one-handed, I pulled off my clothes and crawled into bed, huddling deep into the furs. I felt cold down to the bone.

My hand throbbed with every heartbeat. Through the open

window I could just hear the waves, the black, angry water tearing at the cliffs.

It wasn't as if I didn't know what my mother had planned for me. Her bitterness against my father had hung in the air all my life, like the dampness that no fire could entirely bake out of our hair, our clothes. I knew what he had done, what his father had done. I had the picture in my mind from my mother's words, as if I'd seen it myself—her father's murdered body, the bed furs soaked with his blood, her mother lost to her forever.

She had never once spoken it aloud, but I felt as if I had always known. My mother meant for me to kill my father.

But Accolon needn't have worried. I'd long ago decided I wasn't going to be a blind tool in someone else's hand, a sword with a bitter edge but no mind of its own.

I remembered the one time I'd ever seen my father, the tall blond stranger with the rich clothes, the gold ring on his hand. I wondered if it had troubled him at all to take Gwydre and leave me behind. Or had he found, as my mother had, that a son was an easy thing to give up?

My father had wanted an heir; my mother had wanted a sword arm to deal out her vengeance. Between them they had divided us, my brother and me, like a net full of fish. Now I had neither father nor brother. And when I woke in the morning, I was one teacher less as well. I never saw Accolon again. My mother's face, when she told me he was gone, forbade questions. She barely spoke for a week, and I knew well enough not to bother her. Accolon's name, like Gwydre's, was never mentioned between us again.

I SPENT THAT WINTER WAITING, while the nights grew long and the days short and sunless, while storms kept the sea in a constant gray fury. Waiting for my hand to heal, waiting for the spring to come. Waiting for my seventeenth year, when I would be old enough to join a warband, if I chose. Old enough to leave home. Old enough to travel to my father's court and discover for myself the truth of what he was.

And I knew how I would do it. In the ten years that had passed since the first and last time I'd seen my father, I'd had time to plan exactly what I would do and say when I met him again. One question, that was all I'd need to ask—and then I would know whether or not my father could be trusted.

Spring that year was late in coming. By the time it was warm enough to travel, I was a month past seventeen. I gathered my clothes. I took a handful of coins from the chest in my mother's room and our only horse from the stable.

I didn't tell my mother I was leaving. We'd barely spoken to each other all winter long. Besides, I thought, she would know well enough where I had gone, and why.

16

THREE WEEKS LATER I sat on my horse, looking down on Camelot from the hills to the north.

I knew the city was my father's pride, that he'd built it years ago, at the height of the Saxon wars, abandoning his old court in a Roman town for something smaller, more easily defended, a hill fort like the kings of the old days once had. Circled by its high wall, a neat crown of stone and timber on the flat summit of a hill, Camelot overlooked a green plain of fields and meadows and forest, with a broad river flowing past the foot of the hill to spill into the nearby sea, its clear water mingling with the salty tides.

I led my horse through the open gates in the city wall and into the shouting confusion of a marketplace, wandering between stalls of dyed wool, leatherwork, baskets of apples, squawking chickens, barrels of wine and ale and mead. I stopped only once, by a woodworker's stall, to admire a small dark harp with elegant lines, but I had no money left and nothing to trade. At last I turned toward the center of town and the great hall.

The doorkeeper was drowsing on a bench beside the door, an old man with a thatch of white hair and a scarred brown face like crumpled parchment. I kicked at the leg of the bench to wake him. He snorted, blinked, and peered up at me, unembarrassed. "What is your errand here?"

"I wish to speak with the king." His eyebrows went up and he got to his feet, examining my cloak, covered with mud and grass stains from sleeping by the roadside, the unadorned hilt of my sword, the plain leather trappings of my horse. I returned his gaze steadily, insolently, as if I had nothing on my mind but the great time he was taking doing what I asked.

"What is your business with the king?" he asked doubtfully.

"I wish to speak with him," I said, very softly. And I added, while he was still uncertain, "Tell him his sister's son is here."

Why I said "his sister's son" and not "his son" I'm not sure. Perhaps it just seemed wiser not to reveal everything at once, to keep something for myself. At any rate, the doorkeeper nodded, still eyeing me skeptically, and retreated into the great hall.

He was moving a bit more quickly when he came back. "You are to come in, lord. Here, boy!" A servant boy came running up to take my horse. "Come in, lord, come in."

I followed him into the great hall and past the dais at the far end, through a dark corridor, at last to a small room with one window open to the warm day, red and blue hangings on the walls. A tall, fair-haired man was sitting in a carved wooden chair with his back to the door, one hand scratching the ears of a beautiful dog with golden fur who sat beside him, its head in his lap, its eyes closed in bliss. A scribe who sat nearby was hunched over a tablet in his lap, making quick marks in the wax with a stylus. I opened my mouth and found that there were no words in it. The gatekeeper glanced sideways at me and cleared his throat.

Arthur pushed his chair back as he stood, turning to face the door. "Gwydre! Is Owain with you? We didn't expect you so soon—" He broke off. At last, with a smile trying to break through the astonishment on his face, he spoke again, softly. *"Medraud?"*

The scribe had discreetly gathered up his work and departed; the gatekeeper followed him. "Yes—" My voice came out sounding odd to my own ears and broke off because I couldn't think how to address him; "Uncle" was absurd, but "Father" impossible. Arthur ended my quandary by coming forward, the grin on his face growing wider, and throwing his arms around me in an embrace I was too startled to return.

He drew back but kept both hands on my shoulders, and his delighted smile did not fade. "Medraud. I can hardly believe it—I was expecting Gwydre, and to turn and find you!" Suddenly he was laughing. "'Sister's son,' indeed! Did you say that on purpose, to fool me? Come, sit, you look tired, have you been riding long?" Overwhelmed, I let him settle me in his own chair, as passively as a child. "Are you hungry? I can have them send for some food."

At last I found my tongue, although it stumbled. "No, I'm—I'm not hungry."

I hadn't expected him to act so pleased to see me. I'd expected—I wasn't sure what. But not this. From everything my mother had told me, from the years that had passed without a word since I'd last seen either my father or my brother, I hadn't thought the high king cared, or even remembered, that he had another son.

But however closely I looked, I couldn't find a trace of falseness in Arthur's smile, his welcoming voice. "Well, a drink, then," Arthur insisted. He stuck his head out into the hallway and bellowed for someone to bring some wine, with two cups. As his attention was removed from me for a minute, I found time to recover my senses. After all, I would shortly test the truth of Arthur's fatherly affection. When Arthur came back to sit, like a boy, on the table beside me, I was able to meet his eyes.

He was still smiling. "Well, it is you. And what brings you here? Not that I am not delighted to see you, for any reason. Cafall, stop it—" This to the dog, who sniffed at my boots and thrust a cold nose under my hand. I rubbed the soft ears, but at Arthur's word Cafall went instantly to curl up at his feet, watching me with great dark eyes. "And Gwydre speaks of you often."

I swallowed the uneasy guilt that rose in me at the mention of my brother's name and tried to keep it from showing in my voice. "Gwydre? Where is he?" The one insistent doubt that threatened to spoil the perfection of my plan had always been the thought of my brother. If Gwydre was truly away from the court right now it might be for the best.

Strangely, Arthur looked uncomfortable for a moment. "He is with his foster father—and that is something we will have to discuss, but later—ah, here is the wine!" He was glad of the interruption, and even got up to take the tray from the servingwoman, setting the two wooden goblets and the jug of wine on the table. Having filled both cups, he took one and handed me mine. "You are most welcome here," he said formally, and I smiled in return. "Now, what brings you? Is this a visit, or have you come for a place at my court? And how is Morgan—how is your mother?"

That was the second time he'd seemed uncertain. I felt encouraged. I wasn't the only one unsure of my footing here.

I set my cup down on my knee. "She is well enough. And I have come for a place at your court." I took a breath. "And I have something to ask of you—Father." I said the word deliberately, a challenge, testing my strength, and his. He did not flinch.

"Whatever is in my power."

"Then I ask for my place as your oldest son. I want to be your heir."

He had said it, all those years ago: *"I will take the oldest boy as my heir."* I had never forgotten. This promise of his had become my test. Soon I would know whether the warmth of Arthur's welcome had been honest. In his answer I would learn how much my father cared for me, and for justice.

But even as I waited for Arthur's answer, the thought of Gwydre nagged at me. To give the throne to me, Arthur would have to take it from my brother. In truth, however, Gwydre was Arthur's heir only because of our mother's lie, and surely he knew it as well as I did. I was only trying to set things right.

I kept my eyes on Arthur's face and I saw regret, and something like weariness, but no surprise. He knew. How long had he known that my mother had lied, that I was his oldest son? Why hadn't he come to see me, come to confront my mother, come to fulfill his word? At last he spoke, gently, as though the tone would make up for the words.

"Medraud, that . . . is not within my power."

So it was false after all—the smile, the warmth I had almost let myself trust. Foolish. Foolish and dangerous to have come so close to believing him.

I didn't realize I'd risen until Arthur reached out and closed his hand over my arm, pushing me down again. "Sit, Medraud—please, sit and let me explain. It is not that I don't wish it—"

"I must have been mistaken." I made my voice as cold and sharp as ice splinters. "I asked to see the high king of this land, not a man who has no power over the naming of his own heir!"

His eyes narrowed, but his voice was still soft. "I know you are angry. And I suppose you have a right to be. Will you let me explain?" Grudgingly, I nodded. Arthur put his cup back on the table, sighed, and put both his hands on his knees. "Well, then. To begin with, almost no one at court knows that you and Gwydre are my sons."

He ran a hand through his hair in a gesture I remembered from my mother's hall. "It had to be done that way. You know my wife is a Christian. I've been baptized myself, to please her. And her priests say that my marriage to Morgan—to your mother—was not valid. Because she is my sister, you see, and we were married in the old way. And they say that any child of that marriage would be bastard-born, and no fit king."

"So Gwydre and I must be bastards, then?" I inquired, careful to keep my voice cool. I picked up my goblet again and ran one finger along the rim. "To please your Christian queen?"

"Try to understand, Medraud. My sister Elen—has your mother told you about her?—she has been foster mother to Gwydre. She is married to my pendragon, Owain of Rheged, and most people think Gwydre is their son. And those that know the truth, I can trust to keep their mouths closed on it. I have named Gwydre formally as my heir. And enough debate there was over that, with half the court saying I should divorce Gwen and take a new wife, and the priests shouting that marriage is sacred. But my council has accepted him now, as the son of my oldest sister and my pendragon. And if he looks like me, well, a nephew may look like his uncle, and Elen is as fair as he is, so there's an excuse. You must see that I cannot change it now."

So he had not only lied to me, promising a throne he wouldn't deliver. He'd lied to all of them. His court, his kingdom—founded and built on deception. "*I* am your oldest son!" I protested. "Is there nothing due to me for that?"

Arthur frowned. "You know I have the right, Medraud, to name my own heir. No law says I must choose my oldest son."

True enough—the old law let a king choose any heir from among his sons and grandsons and nephews and cousins. But that wasn't all it said. "And according to the law every heir must be considered," I pointed out. Accolon had taught me more than songs and legends. "What did your council say when you told them of your other . . ." I paused. "Your other sister's son? How many of them spoke for me?"

"I cannot split my court into factions for you!" Arthur's voice sharpened. "I have to keep the truce with the Saxons and find enough for my army to do now that the wars are over. I don't need the court quarreling over the succession like gulls over a scrap of fish!" He softened his tone. "Medraud, it's unfair, I know. There will always be a place for you at my court. If your mother had told me you were the oldest from the first, none of this would have happened. But I only found it out from Gwydre a few years ago, when it was too late to change."

Too late for his convenience, he meant! But I kept the thought from my face. There would be time later to show him what I truly felt. For now I could put on a pleasant counterfeit as easily as Arthur. I nodded solemnly, as if giving him the acceptance he wanted.

"Why did she do that, do you know, Medraud?" Arthur continued. "Was it that she loved you best and didn't want to part with you?" I shook my head. I didn't know why my mother had lied; it wasn't something I could ask her. I'd always suspected she had simply thought Gwydre too weak to act out her vengeance. But now, looking at Arthur's face, I was reminded of how closely my brother resembled him. Perhaps my mother merely hadn't wanted to watch her younger son grow up to look more and more like our father.

Arthur shrugged. "Well, Morgan always had her own reasons

for what she did, even if no one else understood them. Come, you'll want a bath before the evening meal, I expect." At the door he paused, laying a hand on my arm. "As my sister's son you are very welcome here, Medraud. And as my son, though no one knows it but me."

I bowed my head formally, without words.

Arthur showed me to one of the small square chambers off the main hall, and told me it would be mine. Servants brought jugs of steaming water from the kitchens, and soap, and soft linen, and I washed three weeks of grime off my skin. They brought new clothing too, finer than mine: a crimson tunic worked in yellow thread around the throat and wrists, soft leather boots, a silver ring. Gifts from the king, bones to keep the dog from barking.

And did he think it would be enough? Did he think he could deny my birthright, call me bastard-born to my face, refuse to acknowledge me as his son, and that I would take a well-woven tunic and a finely wrought ring in exchange? Did he think I was as helpless as the seven-year-old boy he had left behind?

I had been right not to trust him all those years ago. All his warmth, all his show of affection—false, as shallow as a tide pool on the rocks. Fine words are easy and he could well afford them, as easily as he could afford the new clothing I wore. But I wouldn't be bought off with words or gifts, not when he'd refused the one thing that would have proved his love.

It wasn't only that he'd withheld the throne he'd promised me. My mother, my brother, myself—he'd hidden us away behind his lies as if we were some kind of guilty secret.

And my brother? Did it matter to him? Perhaps, with a throne in his grasp, he didn't mind that our father acted as if he was ashamed of our mother, ashamed of our birth. But I would not sit tamely by and let Arthur deny me, pretend I was never even born.

My father would find it was not so easy to act as though I didn't truly exist. And if he didn't want to give me what was my due, then I would simply take it from him.

But if my mother had imagined that vengeance was going to be as simple as a blade to Arthur's throat—well, she was wrong. Had she expected me to walk into the hall and challenge the high king to single combat? If his warriors didn't laugh themselves sick, they would kill me where I stood.

My mother might well have thought my life would be a cheap price to pay for her vengeance. But I did not agree. No, I would take the blood price Arthur owed for my grandparents' deaths, but not only that. I would also find a way to take the throne he didn't want to give me, the recognition he'd denied me. Once I was king, I wouldn't have to stay in the shadows, watching other people, waiting to see where danger lay. Like a sword in my hand, a throne would be safety.

But taking the throne from Arthur would be complicated. It wasn't just a matter of a sharp blade and a well-timed blow. Warcraft was, after all, about more than handling a sword. It was about strategy.

THAT NIGHT I KNELT AT MY FATHER'S FEET to swear him my loyalty.

By day the great hall had seemed vast and empty. But darkness hid the high corners of the roof and filled up the spaces between the rafters, and people crowded the room with the vivid colors of tunics and cloaks, their bright hair, their pale faces. Wide bowls of hammered bronze, filled with oil and lit with floating wicks, hung from the ceiling and spilled an orange light down in splashes, lighting a pair of laughing eyes, a flash of teeth, a bone-white drinking horn clutched in a hand with a gold ring on one finger. The red war banner with the coiled dragon that hung behind Arthur's chair flickered like a flame. Smells of roasting meat, butter, onions and leeks and fresh bread, stung my nose and dissolved on my tongue with honey-sweet mead and wine from the south.

The words of loyalty came smoothly to my lips as I knelt at Arthur's feet and bowed my head. After all, hadn't he betrayed me first? But when Arthur's hand gathered up the hair from the back of my neck, I froze. When the cold knife brushed my skin I almost trembled.

He could cut my throat easily, and I could do nothing to stop him. If he were wise he would do it. There were stories of lords who killed their subjects, of warriors who attacked the kneeling unarmed man, his back vulnerable, his blood spilling, steaming hot, over the floor.

The knife was so sharp I barely felt the tug as Arthur cut off a lock of my hair close to the skull. "I accept your service," he said clearly. "I will honor your loyalty, provide for you and protect you, take your part against any enemy. I swear it." He held up his hand with the lock of my hair, opened it, and let the hair fall, drifting gently on the air.

Arthur pulled me up and embraced me. Laughing, I felt Arthur's warriors crowd around me, pummeling me in welcome, almost knocking me off my feet. Someone thrust a horn of ale into my hand, and I drank it without a breath. Relief poured through me like floodwater. Uncertainty can kill with anxiety, but anyone can stay on a course, once set there. It doesn't take courage to die defending a barren ridge or flinging yourself against the walls of a hill fort. You only have to decide to do it, decide so utterly that turning back never occurs to you.

The way I had decided that I would betray my father.

At the feast afterward Arthur gave me the place of honor between himself and his wife, Gwenhwyfar. I studied her with interest, this Christian queen, my mother's replacement. Lovely enough, with fine bones and smooth fair hair, blue eyes. She asked pleasant questions about my homeland and my journey—none, I noticed, about my mother. I saw no hint of irony in her eyes or smile when Arthur spoke of me as his nephew.

But I couldn't be sure. It was dark in the hall, and crowded, and I was oddly distracted by glimpses I had of the woman who stood behind her chair. I only saw her out of the corner of my eye, when she leaned forward to offer Gwenhwyfar a new dish or fill her cup with wine: a strong slender hand in a dark brown sleeve, a white curve of cheekbone under dark hair. Something about her intrigued me; maybe it was her stillness as she stood in the shadows, a stillness that broke suddenly into the swift grace of her movements. Like a harp string before it is touched, waiting to burst into sound.

LATER THAT NIGHT, alone in my room, I paced back and forth. The wine and ale I had drunk had made me restless instead of sleepy. My mother and I had drunk wine sometimes, when the southern traders came; some years there were two or three ships, other times years would pass between visits. But Arthur kept a well-stocked larder, apparently.

Arthur. I ran a hand across the back of my neck, as if I expected to feel a brand left there by the touch of his knife. I couldn't stop thinking of him—not his face, not his eyes, but the gentleness of his hand as he held the knife so that the blade barely touched my skin.

To try and shake Arthur from my mind, I thought again of the woman at the feast, behind the queen's chair. I would find out who she was tomorrow, I promised myself. But when I heard a faint sound and looked up, she was standing in the doorway to my room, as if my thoughts had conjured her.

"Is there anything else you require this night, my lord?"

Her voice was low, quiet, respectful. She'd startled me so badly that I almost snapped at her to go away, leave me alone. But something about her caught my attention. Maybe it was the edge of amusement in her voice, so faint I wasn't sure I'd heard it right. The hallway outside my room was dark, and I found myself wanting to see her face. "Who sent you?" was all I could think of to ask.

"The king, your . . . uncle." There was all the irony in her voice that had been missing from Gwenhwyfar's. I could see the soft folds of her skirt, her hands. Impatient, I snatched up a candle from the chest and took a step forward, letting light fall on her face.

"What is your name?" I demanded.

"Gwenhwyfach."

The name and the face together were startling in their familiarity. "You are the queen's—" What? Distant cousin, bastard daughter?

"Sister. Our father is the same."

That explained it. She was years younger than Gwenhwyfar, who in turn was younger than Arthur, so her age was not much greater than my own. Her hair was darker than her sister's, her eyes the deep brown of drowned leaves, under brows too straight and thick for beauty. But the fine bones of the face were the same, and the full mouth.

She let me stare for a minute, and then bowed her head. "If there is nothing else I can do for you tonight, my lord, my mistress expects me." She turned as if to go, but I caught her with a question.

"Do you like serving your sister as your mistress?"

She looked back over her shoulder. "No more than you will like serving your brother as your king."

She knew what Arthur had said no one knew—this serving girl, the queen's half sister. How had she learned that Arthur was our father, mine and Gwydre's? And what did she want to gain by dangling her knowledge, like bait, before me?

"How do you know?"

One corner of her mouth lifted, not quite a smile. "There's not much at this court that I do not know."

An alliance? Was that what she was offering me, this bastard-born servant? I was intrigued by the way she didn't smile, the way she let her silence be a challenge between us. *I have something you want,* her face declared. *Show me what you'll give for it.* She was like a trader dangling a chunk of amber or a deep blue sapphire carelessly between his fingers, telling you by his very refusal to name a price just how valuable it is.

It was a relief to face someone without any pretense of love or loyalty, only the balance of a bargain holding us together. But if her knowledge of the court was her half of the bargain, what was mine? I decided to try and see what price she would hold out for.

"Who else knows that Arthur is our father?"

"Not many."

"Who?"

She lifted her eyebrows a little, expectantly. I stepped back and let her into the room, shutting the door behind us. Calmly she took a seat on a chest, tucking her skirts around her feet. I hadn't expected her to tell me her information without naming her price, but she began talking, her voice matter-of-fact.

"Owain Pendragon, of course. His wife too, but she never comes south to the court. I think the king's cousins know, at least Gawain, the oldest. No one else."

"Not the queen?"

"Gwenhwyfar doesn't know." I think she saw skepticism on my face, for she continued. "At first Arthur didn't tell her that Owain was raising his son for him because he didn't want to call her barren to her face. If she'd ever had a son, Gwydre would have stayed north and inherited all Owain Pendragon's lands. But she never did. And by the time everyone knew she'd never bear a child, they all thought Gwydre was Owain's son. By then Arthur didn't want to tell her he'd lied."

It was as if she'd laid the jewel in my hand, with a look that mocked prices and bargains and trades. If it was true—and it rang true as silver, every word—she'd given me a stunning gift.

"Why are you telling me?" She had me at a disadvantage, pretending she wanted nothing in return. If she'd held out her hand for gold, or hinted at a favor she'd need in the future, I would have known how to treat her. But she eluded the trap by simply smiling at me.

"What else do you want to know?"

Very well. I would accept her on her own terms. If she could tell me more things like that she could name her price when she chose. When I was king I'd give her whatever she asked.

17

OVER THE NEXT WEEK I watched Gwenhwyfach carefully, judging my new ally's worth. There was a surprising beauty in her dark eyes, in the thick hair she often let fall like a curtain to hide her face. But you had to look closely to see it. And looking closely at Gwenhwyfach, I discovered, was something no one ever did.

As she moved quietly on the queen's errands she kept her head bowed, her face shuttered and dull. In her dark brown dress she all but vanished in the shadows. Even the other servants barely noticed her.

No one remembered to drop his voice when she came near. No one bothered to hide a meaningful glance from her sight, or wipe emotion from his face in her presence.

Gwenhwyfach had been more than right when she said there was not much at the court that she did not know. And she told it all to me: family histories, ancient feuds, new alliances, who was whose cousin or brother-in-law, which boys were not their fathers' sons, whose wife's affections had wandered into whose bed.

As she sat on a chest in my room or at the foot of my bed, talking, her face would light up, vivid, startlingly alive. She had nothing like her sister's golden sunlit beauty—this was darker, deeper. Like a coal that looks dull and dusty black, but splits open at a touch to show its glowing red heart.

Among other things, she pointed out my mother's cousins before I met them. The youngest of them, Gareth, had just joined Arthur's warband; he was not much older than I was. But it was two weeks before I met my closest relative; Gwydre was traveling with his foster father. When at last I heard he was returning, I waited for him nervously. Gwydre was my brother, my twin. But he was also Arthur's heir, and I had come to take away that place.

My father had called me to him so that we could meet Gwydre together. I wanted to pace the room, but I would not display my nerves before Arthur. I sat quietly. As we talked there were footsteps in the hall and a voice, high-pitched as a boy's, called out, "You wanted to see me?"

As Arthur was greeting his heir, I observed them, making swift comparison in my mind between the seven-year-old boy I remembered and the seventeen-year-old man before me. He still resembled our father, though Gwydre's face was thinner, his hair lighter, his eyes nearly as blue as Gwenhwyfar's. He looked *young,* I thought in astonishment. I had been preparing myself to meet someone much different from the picture I carried in my head, and here was a boy with the eager smile and chatter of a child.

Arthur was smiling at something Gwydre was telling him about the journey, and he put a hand on Gwydre's shoulder, turning him toward me. "Here's someone for you to meet," he said. I rose to my feet.

Gwydre didn't recognize me. With a look of expectant curiosity, he waited for Arthur to tell him who I was.

Arthur realized this a few seconds too late. "Well, why should I expect you to know each other? It has been ten years since you were together. This is Medraud, Gwydre. He arrived here only two weeks ago."

For a moment Gwydre blinked in blank surprise. Then he shouted, "Medraud!" and threw himself at me, pounding my back in his enthusiasm. Laughing, I held on to him to keep my balance.

It was all right, after all; he remembered me, and everything would be like it used to be between us.

Grinning, Gwydre pulled back to look at me. "I don't believe it. You here, of all places! Why did you come?"

"Well, you couldn't expect me to stay in Cornwall forever! I thought it was time I saw you again, and you showed no signs of coming to see me. Do you miss it, though?" I asked, sitting down again as my brother leaned against the arm of Arthur's chair. "I remember how you loved the sea."

"Well, it's been so long—I hardly remember it now. But I'm glad you're here! Have you seen everything? May I show him the town, uncle?"

"I've been here two weeks," I protested, but Arthur laughed and nodded.

"Remember," our father said, coming to meet us at the door. "Outside of this room you are not brothers, only cousins. You both know the reason for this." He looked sharply at both of us, a bit harder at me. "Of course," Gwydre said cheerfully, pulling me out of the room before I had time to do more than nod. Which was just as well.

"HE DOESN'T EVEN *CARE*," I brooded to Gwenhwyfach that night. She sat on a chest in my room, her head bent over an intricate belt she was embroidering for the queen. Bright silk leaves and flowers grew quickly under her fingers. "Our father will not acknowledge us openly," I complained, "and it means *nothing* to him. He calls him 'uncle'!"

"What did you expect?" Gwenhwyfach didn't look up. "What does he have to gain by protesting? The kingdom will come to him one way or another, as the king's son or the king's sister's son. You are the only one who is hurt by this."

"I am his brother—he might care that I am being denied my rightful place!"

She kept her head bowed so that I could barely see the sharp smile on her face. "You are his brother—how much do you care that you are trying to supplant him?"

Usually I appreciated Gwenhwyfach's subtle malice. Just as no one else saw her quiet beauty, I was the only one who ever heard her slyly sharp tongue.

But I didn't much care for it when it was directed at me. I slammed my cup down on the table, spilling some of Arthur's good wine in a red wave over my hand. "I only want what is rightfully mine!"

"Of course, Medraud. I was not accusing you."

Her tone was mild, innocent, but a restless silence stretched out between us. I traced patterns with my finger in the pool of spilled wine. The throne could only go to one man. Surely I had a better right to it than my younger brother, who was only the heir because of my mother's scheme. "Besides," I added abruptly, "Gwydre hardly wants to be a king. He'd rather be a jeweler or a metalworker, that's what he cares about. A king making brooches and rings and harness fastenings!"

The last place Gwydre had taken me that afternoon had been a jeweler's workroom. My brother was well known there; the craftsmen greeted him warmly by name, and only a few, I noticed, by title. On a table near a window, among bits of scrap glass, coils of thin gleaming wire, fine brushes, and small knives lay a ring brooch. On its ends intricate knotwork twined around the bodies of bright green birds.

"Good, no one touched it. What do you think?" Gwydre looked at me with a proud smile.

"It's yours?"

"Yes, mine. It's almost done; I just have to touch up the enameling a bit. Do you like it?"

I stared at him. "Is this a king's work?"

Gwydre looked embarrassed. "It'll be *years* before I am a king, Medraud. Why think about it now? Don't you like the brooch?"

"It's beautiful," I said honestly. Gwydre smiled.

"I started doing this sort of thing years ago, with my mother, but the craftsmen here know so much more."

I felt as if he had suddenly turned and hit me in the stomach—wounded, out of breath. "With your . . . mother?"

"Well, my foster mother really—Elen. You'll have to come

north with me sometime and meet her. You'll like her, Medraud, she is our mother's sister, you know."

I nodded, but I didn't speak. Gwydre didn't seem to notice. He turned his attention back to the brooch, picking it up delicately between two fingers and holding it to the light. "Medraud, could you find your way back, do you think? I can finish this before dark if I get started now."

"I've been here two weeks," I said dryly, "and I'm not blind or a fool."

Gwydre smiled vaguely and nodded.

"Good-bye, cousin." I laid a breath of emphasis on the final word, watching to see how he would react. But Gwydre only bent lovingly over his work, humming to himself.

I told this to Gwenhwyfach, who smiled indulgently. "No one can tear him away from his metalwork once he's started."

"And Arthur thinks an *artist* will be able to rule his kingdom?" I asked in disbelief.

Gwenhwyfach shrugged. "He's young yet. Arthur thinks he will learn."

"Does the rest of the court think that?"

"Most of them." Her hands slowed over her work. I leaned forward, elbows on my knees, to listen. "Owain, of course, supports Gwydre, and most of the warriors follow Owain's lead. But I think Gawain has his doubts, and maybe his brothers. He's from the north, and he doesn't have much use for artists." She smiled. "A lot of the northern lords weren't fond of Owain not so long ago. He's from the north, you know. He came south to fight Arthur and wound up serving him. The northern lords were a long time forgetting that. Some of them never did."

Another gem of knowledge laid in my lap, a glistening fact to add to the pattern I was building. I smiled at her in pure pleasure, her earlier taunt forgiven. "I think the gods sent you as a gift to me," I told her. "You don't tell these things to anyone else, do you?" It was an alarming thought.

"No one else ever asks me." She began to sew again, her long needle stabbing angry stitches through the wool.

"More fools they."

"I'm the one they think is a fool." She looked up quickly, one corner of her mouth lifting just a little in a smile with plenty of bitterness behind it. "Or deaf and blind as stone. They think I have no eyes or ears, only hands to fetch and carry and sew and mend." She hooked a length of silk behind one tooth and bit it off short. "I must go; she wants this tonight."

But I stopped her before she reached the door, laying a hand on her shoulder. The rough cloth of her dress slipped a little on her warm, smooth skin as she turned to face me. She was just my height, her questioning eyes level with my own.

"I know," I told her. I knew she had eyes and ears, a mind and heart. I knew she wasn't what they thought her, any more than I was the meek and dutiful nephew Arthur thought me.

The two of us together made a dark knot of shadow at the bright heart of Arthur's court. She was my ally, my fellow conspirator; she was the only one at that court I never had to lie to.

But it was more than that, what I felt for her. She understood what it was like to stay in the shadows, ignored and passed over by the family who should have defended and protected. And unlike the rest of the court, unlike even my brother, she was not dazzled by the golden light of Arthur and his queen. She knew the truth, the same truth I did. Clear-eyed, she saw the lies, the dark secrets behind the throne.

I touched my fingers gently to the soft skin over her cheekbones, now flushed red. She was the one who kissed me, her lips warm against mine. The queen's shadow sister, the dark twin, my Gwen.

18

IT WAS A WAR OF WHISPERS I meant to wage against my father, and it was Gwydre who'd given me my first weapon. Carefully choosing my listeners, I would wonder aloud if the king's heir wasn't a little too interested in metalwork and jewelry, and not enough in politics and war. I had fought a few practice bouts with Gwydre, and before long he'd been panting as if he'd run a mile. If he were one of Gwyn ap Nudd's warriors whose shining faces alone could terrify their enemies, all would be well; but as a king leading his army into battle, he would be hopeless.

For this position I found supporters, but too lukewarm for my taste. Their attitude, as Gwenhwyfach had said, was that Gwydre was young and still had time to learn. But it didn't hurt to set them wondering if there were any other relative the king might have chosen as his heir. I felt a twinge of guilt now and then for maligning my brother so publicly. But after all it was the truth and no more that I said. And Gwydre, absorbed in his metals and paints, almost never heard the rumors around the court.

Gwenhwyfach had given me my next weapon on my first night at the court. It was a powerful one, but I had to bide my time until I could use it to best effect. While waiting, I discovered my most dangerous enemy.

Arthur was more inclined to trust me than was wise. He would give me nothing of what I was due, but in his pride he would not believe that his own kin would work against him. And the whispers around the court were too soft to reach his ear. After all, who will say straight out to a king that his heir is a fool? But Owain Pendragon, Gwydre's foster father, was another matter.

When Gwydre introduced us, we took each other's measure, like two wolfhounds smelling a fight. I knew Arthur had told him who I was and what I wanted. And I had heard enough stories about him—the hero of the Saxon wars, and the commander of the Ravens, the best warband in Arthur's army—to make me wonder if he was as fearsome an opponent off the battlefield as on.

I suspected so. He was slight, dark, with dull black hair neatly combed back from his clean-shaven face. The ring brooch holding his cloak at the shoulder had, if you looked closely, two ravens on the ornamented ends. He gave me one sharp glance from head to toe and then a friendly smile.

"Since you are my foster son's brother, I think there must be some relationship between us. Welcome to Camelot."

I smiled back and accepted what he offered—not peace, but the smooth appearance of pleasantry. "Since you are my mother's sister's husband, I think we must indeed be related. I am glad to meet you."

I think Owain guessed fairly quickly that I was the source of the doubts and dissatisfactions that were stirring, like flies in August, around the court. But he couldn't prove anything, or do anything without proof. Out of his earshot I frowned and murmured, and whispered my disquieting suspicions, and brooded on the unshakable triumvirate of Arthur and Gwenhwyfar and Owain. Those three at the heart of the kingdom made my best efforts almost worthless; the mere sight of them silenced all doubts, healed all division. But they were not invulnerable, and I knew a way to unsettle at least one of their hearts.

I was sitting with Arthur and Gwenhwyfar, Gwydre and Owain, and my cousin Gawain, a great hulking redheaded bear of a man with a trace of northern accent and a scorn for anything southern that was tempered only by his utter loyalty to Arthur. I was picking at the strings of the new harp Arthur had given me—the very one I'd admired in the marketplace my first day in Camelot. Gwenhwyfar was idly pulling a piece of bread to crumbs on the table, and Arthur and Owain and Gawain were discussing a Saxon warband that was threatening the treaty peace. Arthur looked up.

"It's pretty enough, Medraud, but why don't you play something more cheerful? Come, Owain, cousin, we'll leave; we're interrupting the music. Gwydre, no—" for my brother looked hopefully at the door, as if he might escape. Talk of politics always bored him. "You need to know about this. Stay and amuse your aunt, Medraud."

It was perfect. After they left, I touched a few of the harp strings lightly and looked at Gwenhwyfar with a guileless smile. "How shall I amuse you then? With music or conversation? I am at your command." If Owain had been there he might have seen through it, but she only laughed.

"Tell me the name of that song you were playing. What is it? I never heard it before."

"I don't know the name. It's an old tune. My uncle said—" I stopped, chuckled, and looked at her as though to share a smile. She looked back expectantly, waiting for the joke to be explained.

"Well, we don't have to play that game when we're alone, do we? I've gotten so used to lying, I forget when I can speak the truth."

"What . . . lie, Medraud?" Now there was no smile. She sat upright, her face grave.

I continued to play the innocent, lounging back in my chair. "Why, that he is my uncle. We both know he is my father." I grinned inside myself, but kept solicitude on my face. "Surely he told you that I am Gwydre's brother?"

Gwenhwyfar rose quickly and clumsily to her feet. "This is not true, they would not both have lied to me." She was not so beautiful now, her face too pale, her mouth struggling with words. "Gwydre is Owain's son."

I rose also, the concerned nephew. "My lady—Gwenhwyfar—are you all right? I never would have told you, but I thought surely you knew." She caught at my arm, but not to steady herself—to keep me at arm's length from her.

"You are lying! Arthur would have told me—"

"Lying? Look at Gwydre's face if you need proof of his parentage—"

Her eyes went suddenly to something over my shoulder. I turned; Arthur was standing in the doorway.

It couldn't have been better timed if I had planned it myself. With Arthur before her, Gwenhwyfar could not fail to see that Gwydre was a thinner, frailer version of our father. I expected tears or rage. But she only gathered herself in, and with a look at Arthur colder than north wind, she walked through the doorway, one shoulder up and her head turned aside as if her husband were some slimy thing she didn't wish to touch.

Arthur did not go after her—a wise decision, I thought. He turned to me instead. "What is this, Medraud?" For the first time, looking at him, I remembered what his father had been—tyrant, warlord, murderer. If I had not had my defense ready, I might have quailed before the threat in his voice.

I did have it ready, however, and spread my hands in a gesture of bewilderment. "I only mentioned that you were my father and Gwydre's, and she called me a liar!"

"You told her that? I told you never to speak of it!"

"I thought she knew! You said you had told those you trusted, and I thought surely your *wife*—"

"You should not have done this."

"How was I to know?" I filled my face with injured innocence. "Father, I'm truly sorry she is angry. But if you had told me she didn't know, I would never have said a word! How could I know you had not told your own wife?" I made my voice pathetic. "Sometimes I get tired of the lies."

If I had been Arthur, I would have killed me then and there. But kindness was Arthur's weakness. He could commit wrongs, but he could not forget them, and once accused, he was all too ready to believe himself guilty. "I suppose you were not to know," he said, magnanimously forgiving. "I'll go after her, explain." He looked at me sharply. "But you are to speak to *no one* of your blood unless I give you leave!"

He left. I picked up Gwenhwyfar's cup of wine and swallowed what was left, to celebrate my first real victory.

Arthur made his peace with Gwenhwyfar somehow. After all, it was what he did best. But I hoped that the whisper of suspicion in her mind would never be truly stilled. Now she knew he had lied to her once, and Owain also; she didn't have the temper to forget it completely.

I waited patiently, watching for my next battlefield. Though when I first saw it, I almost didn't recognize it.

It was a sweltering day, too hot for helmet and mail, and I was out in the practice yard trying to keep Gareth, Gawain's youngest brother, from impaling me with a spear. My cousin was slow-witted and dull as a northern winter, but good with weapons and a little overenthusiastic about practice. I couldn't land a blow on him.

Jumping aside as Gareth stabbed at my knees, I grabbed for the spear, but missed and cursed, and became aware that someone was watching us. I glanced up for an instant, and there was a brown-haired woman, in middle age, a stranger, standing on the edge of the practice yard. She looked a bit travel-stained and worn, and she was eyeing me curiously.

Gareth's spear came within a few inches of my ribs, and brought my attention back to matters at hand. But when I heard a servant boy yell Owain's name and saw him point at the woman, I looked up in surprise. Gareth hooked his foot behind my ankle and yanked me off balance. Flat on my back, I saw his spear come in with frightening speed and stop with the point just a few inches from my throat.

I slapped the spear away. What was he laughing at, as if it were a heroic thing to take advantage of a moment's inattention? And there was Gawain, laughing too, shouting to his younger brother that he should have spitted me like a pig for daydreaming during a fight. I longed to give Gareth a clout, just with the hilt of my sword, that would knock the grin off his face, but I wanted to know about Owain's visitor more than I wanted to teach my cousin a lesson in courtesy.

Owain was at the woman's side now, but he glanced over and shouted at Gareth and me to put on our helmets, as if we were common soldiers. "I've finished," I said, coming up to them. "Who's your visitor?"

"A messenger." Owain didn't quite say that he didn't intend to discuss his affairs before me, but it couldn't have been clearer. "Come inside, Luned, I'll hear you there."

The name meant nothing to me, but I stored it carefully in my mind; it might prove useful someday to know something Owain clearly didn't want to discuss before his warriors. I looked after them thoughtfully as the woman followed him inside. Maybe Gwenhwyfach would know who she was.

Gwenhwyfach often made her way to my room after her mistress had gone to bed. Usually she came so quietly that even though I was listening for her, I wasn't aware of her until she stood in the doorway. But this evening I heard quick footsteps slapping against the floor. She swung into my room and stood glaring at me, breathing hard and too angry to speak.

"Gwen?" Astonished, I came to her side. For her I would even be humble; she was an ally I could not afford to lose. "What's wrong? Have I—"

"Bitch!" she spat furiously. She moved away from me, biting off her words and spitting them out as though she hated the taste. "I'll *kill* her—to call me that—after all this time, does she think she can—"

"Gwenhwyfach!" I grabbed her shoulder and spun her around to face me. I saw the bloody tracks of nails across her cheek, the bruise already darkening. "Did *she* do that? Gwenhwyfar?"

"Oh, she did it—my sweet sister!" She wrenched away from my hand and threw herself down on the chest by the window. Arms crossed, she stared blindly at the wall opposite, trembling with rage. "I am the daughter of a king as she is, and all my life I have braided her hair, and served her meals, and called her *my lady,* and heard her condescend and be *so* kind—"

"Gwen!" I came to kneel beside the chest. "I know how it is to be set aside for your own kin, you know I do. Tell me what happened."

She took a breath, forcing herself to be calmer. "She had a fight with Owain, I think. He's off to the north again, and for some reason she didn't want him to go. I started to comb out her hair, and all of a sudden she asked if I was going to you tonight. When I didn't answer she called me a whore, and she moved her head, and the comb caught in a tangle and pulled some hair out. She called me clumsy, a fool, and she hit me—" She shivered. "If I hadn't left the room I would have killed her. To call me that, when I have kept her secret all these years . . ."

"What secret?" Was this something she hadn't told me? Did she keep things from me too?

Gwenhwyfach hesitated.

"What loyalty do you owe her now?" I coaxed, touching her bruised cheek gently.

She laughed angrily. Her eyes still looked savagely at nothing, as if she saw her sister across the room. "Call *me* a whore! When she and the great lord Owain Pendragon . . ."

It was too good to be true. Gwenhwyfar and Owain? A way to wound both Arthur and Gwenhwyfar, *and* destroy my greatest enemy at the court?

"Gwen, do you mean it? The queen and—"

"And the great Pendragon," she finished for me. "Oh, they are discreet about it, but I know. I've carried their messages for them. She begged me, and I swore not to tell."

More lies at the heart of that perfect kingdom, that perfect marriage. But I frowned at Gwenhwyfach as a disquieting thought struck me.

"Why didn't you tell me before?"

She pulled her hands out of mine. "What promise have I made to tell you everything I know?"

I let go of my indignation. Gwenhwyfach was not Arthur, to believe herself guilty because I told her so. If I reprimanded her now, I might lose the chance to hear more of what she knew. "No promise, love. But you've told me now, and I thank you. Would you swear to it?"

"Swear? Don't you believe—"

"To Arthur."

Comprehension lit her eyes. "Oh. No, I would not."

I sat back on my heels. Was she going to ruin everything now by defying me? "Why not? Do you love your sister so much you fear to hurt her?"

"Don't be a fool." Her lips twitched with exasperation. "My word against hers? Do you think I want to be banished for false swearing against the queen?"

She was right. "Well then, not that. If we caught them together—"

"And what if? Fool, if you think Owain couldn't fight his way out of any trap."

"Not if he was unarmed, in bed with her."

"He always takes his sword."

He would. He was cautious as a cat, that one. "Well, I will think of something." I moved to sit beside her on the chest, and gently touched her bruised, bloody face. I had never loved her so well as now, when she had given my weapon of revenge into my hands. The tears of rage in her eyes made them darker, deeper. I tasted salt blood on her lips.

Later that night, as she lay warm beside me under the bed furs, her back against my chest, her soft hair brushing my face, she sighed. Her voice was faint, so quiet I had to strain to hear her, even as close as I was. "She's taken everything," Gwenhwyfach whispered. "All my life . . ."

She turned beneath my arm so that she lay on her back, staring up at the ceiling. "She would be shocked, do you know that, Medraud? If she knew where I was, what I'd told you. She thinks she can trust me!" A low laugh shook her. "After all she's done . . ."

And was it any different from what Arthur thought of me? It was the worst insult of all, worse than the blow across her face, worse than Arthur's refusal to acknowledge me as his son: that neither of them dreamed we might be other than dumb and blindly loyal as dogs.

I lifted a hand to brush back a strand of her hair that clung to the dried blood on her face. Her eyes were somber, almost sad. It was as if her rage had vanished, drowned in a strange, deep sorrow. It puzzled me.

"What will you do, Medraud?"

Was she only uncertain about our next step? "I don't know yet," I confessed. I kissed the soft skin of her shoulder. "We can't accuse either of them without proof, and how to get it . . ." It was maddening to have the perfect weapon in my hands and no way to use it.

"Promise me . . ."

Her voice faltered. I wanted to bring joy back to her face, or at least anger. Anything but this uncanny grief, as if she'd lost herself.

"I promise," I told her. "I promise you she'll suffer."

19

HE NEXT MORNING I WENT TO SEE ARTHUR. He would always make time for me when I asked, and look glad to see me, as though he thought that would make up for his refusal to grant me my rights. I asked a few meaningless questions, and let him see I was nervous. "What is it?" he said at last.

Hesitant, I began to tap my fingers against my leg, avoiding his eyes. "There is something. About my lady Gwenhwyfar. I don't know if I should tell you."

"Well, decide." He smiled a little to take the sharpness out of his words.

"She and Owain Pendragon, Father. They—" I faltered, as if the news were too terrible to speak. "They have betrayed you."

As the silence between us grew thicker, I had to look up at him at last. There was no change in his face, except for a slight thinning of his mouth.

"Well," he said dryly, "do you think I don't have eyes?"

"What?"

"I have known that for years." I felt a touch of panic, as my careful plan started to unravel in my hands. "Nothing will come of it. If you accused them, you would have to prove it to my satisfaction, and that will never be done." His tone was thoughtful. "But I wonder why you came to tell me this."

"I thought you should know—I had no idea you would not *care*—" I was floundering, grabbing at excuses.

"What trouble are you trying to raise, Medraud? To break me away from Owain—was that your plan?"

"I only wanted—"

"I think I know." Arthur sighed and rubbed his forehead. "You wanted my kingdom, and since I wouldn't give it to you, you decided to destroy it. Owain has told me of rumors around the court, but I would not believe they came from my own son."

After seventeen years of silence, after lying about my birth, after denying me my right to be considered for the throne—*now* he wanted me to be his son? But I still kept my face innocent, hoping to recover some of the ground I had lost. "Will you take Owain's word over mine?" I protested.

"I will take his word." Arthur's voice sharpened. "For he is my friend, and loyal, and able to think of something other than himself. All of which you are not." An old sadness softened his eyes, though it didn't touch the stern line of his mouth. "As selfish as your mother," he said quietly. "I shouldn't have left you with her so long."

Suddenly I cared very little about recovering lost ground. What right had he to judge my mother, when he was the one who'd betrayed and abandoned her? "Don't speak of her," I snapped. "You cast her off. You cast us both off—we were no use to you, so you threw us away. Can you call me selfish, when you care for nothing but your kingdom—what *you* have made, what belongs to *you*—"

"Enough!" Arthur took a step forward, but I met his angry gaze with my own. All this time Arthur had been living in some dream where I was his dutiful son. He'd never once looked closely enough to see me for what I was. Now he could not avoid the truth, and I knew his façade of fatherly affection would never survive it. It was pure black joy to face him as an enemy at last.

Arthur took a quick breath, as though trying for patience. "I did not cast your mother off, Medraud, whatever she may have told you."

I remembered my mother, those days when she seemed not to see me or anything around her, when she would talk on and on, her voice spinning grief out of the air—her father murdered, her mother raped; her own husband, her own brother, turned against her. Once she had put her hand in the fire, holding it there until I screamed. But when she turned to face me, she was smiling. "You see," she had said, "fire doesn't hurt," though the blisters on her hand were weeping blood.

I knew well enough that she had been ready to sacrifice me for her vengeance. I knew too that she lied when it suited her. But the one thing I had always been sure of was her pain. "She told me the truth," I said savagely. "How you let a murderer stay at your court, and were too much of a coward to avenge your own mother. I have always known your family meant nothing to you."

Arthur's face didn't change. "I had that argument with your mother, Medraud. I will not have it now with you," he said shortly. "If I chose to let my bard stay at my court, that was my right." He looked sternly at me, reproving and regal. "This is the end of your rumors and whispers. If I hear more of this, you will leave."

I sneered at him. "You can't banish me. You would have to declare the cause before the full court. Would you tell them all that your wife is a whore and your heir a fool?" I lifted my face to his raised fist but made no defense, and he dropped it again. "You could take a knife to my throat, Father, or tell Owain to do it for you if you can't stomach blood. But if you don't, I'll leave when I am ready."

I turned on my heel and left him there.

I paced through the darkness of the great hall and out into the sunlight. I was as tired as if I'd been in a sword fight and had nearly come out the worse.

Which, to be honest, I had. Despite the exhilaration of knowing that the lies between myself and my father were gone, it was not good strategy to have revealed myself so early. A break between Arthur and Owain would do me no good if both were my enemies.

Then I slowed my steps as an idea came to me. Arthur was no longer my ally, but it might not be too late to make myself a new one. It would be a gamble; if it failed, I might well be exiled, if not killed outright. But I had been waiting and whispering for long enough. It was time to throw the dice and see what my luck would bring.

Gwenhwyfach agreed to tell me the next time her sister and Owain planned to meet, her smile lighting her eyes with malice. While I waited, I avoided Arthur and the queen. Arthur seemed content to leave me alone, which was all I wanted from him. I spent my time doing a new kind of whispering.

To a few I chose myself, I murmured my suspicions that the two closest to the king had betrayed him. From their reactions, I saw that it was not entirely unthought of. I would not tell the king, I said, without direct proof, but the next time they were together, we would catch them and accuse them. Then, maybe, the king could marry again and breed an heir of his own blood, I told them, nodding wisely.

I chose them well; none of them stalked away in anger to warn Owain or the king. Instead, with worried faces, they listened and swore secrecy. There were four besides me in my little band of spies, all young, not too intelligent, and easy to persuade. Two brothers, Sinnoch and Baedan, and Sel ap Selgi, and the fourth my cousin Gareth. I hesitated over including him, wanting no one near Owain's equal with a sword to be there that night, but decided that among so many bunglers one good blade would make little difference.

Owain had disappeared for a few weeks, off on some errand to the north; it seemed the messenger I'd seen in the practice yard had been from his wife. Which might, I supposed, have something to do with the queen's foul temper that night. At any rate, it gave me plenty of time to arrange things as I wanted them.

The very day of his return, Gwenhwyfach stopped me on my way back to the hall from the practice yard. "Tonight," she said softly, her hand on my arm. The bruise on her face had faded to yellow, and she wore a new dress, dark red—Gwenhwyfar's gift, an apology. "After Arthur is asleep, they are to meet in the room they keep for guests. I'm to bring him to her. I'll tell you when."

I went to talk to the captain of the watch and found out which men were to stand guard at Camelot's gate that night. They were glad to hear that the schedule had been changed and they would not be on duty after all.

I was awake when Gwenhwyfach came to my doorway, a candle in her hand. I wondered if my eyes looked as bright as hers in the weird shadowy light. "I am going to Owain now," she whispered.

"Don't hurry." I found my sword belt, stood up to buckle it on, slid my knife into its sheath. "I have to get everyone together. And Gwen—" I stopped her at the door. "Tell him to bring his sword."

She went still under my hand. "Not to bring it, you mean."

"Tell him to bring it." Her eyes were doubtful. "Gwen, trust me, love. I have something more planned for them than just an accusation and trial." I gave her a quick kiss. "Tell him Gwenhwyfar said to be sure to bring his sword."

She hesitated, nodded, and moved quickly away. I picked up a small bundle of my possessions that I had packed beforehand. I thought for a moment about taking the harp, but it was too big; someone would be bound to notice it. And at any rate it had been Arthur's gift; I would take nothing of his with me. I hurried to wake Gareth and told him to get the others. We met outside the guest room door.

I looked them over. Pale in the dark, sleepy-eyed, stupid, every one armed. Gareth couldn't stop yawning. I drew them back around a corner and set Sel to watch for the pendragon.

We were barely in place when Sel jerked his head back around the corner, nodding wildly. I made calming gestures with both hands, and as we listened, I could hear cat-soft footfalls and the shifting and creaking of a sword belt.

We waited until we heard the door open, and a murmured welcome. Then the door shut again and I pushed Gareth forward. He gaped at me, but I hissed, "Go on!" and he stumbled forward and hit the door planks hard with the hilt of his sword.

"Traitor! Open the door!" he shouted.

That set them off. They crowded around the door, yelling and hammering. I waited behind to see what would happen.

The door flung outward with the force of Owain's shoulder behind it. He slammed it shut again as soon as he was clear, his blade swinging out in an arc that knocked Sinnoch's sword aside and cut a deep gash across his upper arm. Sinnoch screamed and dropped his sword to clamp his fingers over the spurting blood.

Owain's sword rang against Sel's with enough force to knock him off balance and into the wall, and in the same motion Owain twisted to kick Baedan in the knee, and stamped hard on his sword hand as he went down. His blade went up again to meet Gareth's as my cousin stepped forward, swinging his sword down in an overhead stroke with plenty of power behind it.

I decided it was time to interfere. I stepped behind Gareth before his sword could come down and shoved him hard. Gareth fell forward onto Owain's sword. It was hardly a thrust; the pen-dragon even stepped back a pace, as if he wanted to prevent it if he could. I tripped Sel and kicked him in the stomach as he fell. Owain sank with Gareth to the ground, trying to ease him off the sword blade, as Baedan stumbled up to stand over them, lifting his weapon. I grabbed the neck of his tunic and slammed the hilt of my sword against his skull. Baedan fell forward with a moan, his sword thudding loudly against the wooden floor.

Owain stood up, letting Gareth's body slide off his blade. I heard my cousin's last breath rasp in his throat. Sel was curled into a ball on the floor, not moving. On his knees, wide-eyed, Sinnoch looked back and forth from Gareth's body to me. "You," he whimpered. "You . . ."

I moved the tip of my blade an inch in the direction of his throat. He swallowed and was silent. I seized Owain's arm.

"Come on, man, the entire court must have heard them. Hurry!"

Owain stood rooted. "I can't leave her—Gwen!"

"She's safer without you. Come on!" I hauled him forward. He stumbled once, and came after me as the first people began to appear.

We ran through the great hall, dodging the sleepers around the hearth, and out into the courtyard. The horse I had saddled earlier stood outside the stables, chewing its bit. I wanted him on the horse and gone, but Owain turned to face me.

"How did you know?"

"Gareth wanted me to join them. I warned the queen not to call you to her tonight. Didn't she tell you?" With satisfaction I saw the look of betrayal on his face. "But when I heard them gathering in the hallway I came to see what was happening. Lucky for you that I did!"

There was no answering smile. "Medraud," he said soberly. "I have misjudged you. I owe you my life—"

"Fool, there's no *time* for this!" I shoved him toward the horse, in agony in case we should be found and captured and he should learn what he really owed me. "You've killed one of the king's cousins, do you want to stand there and be taken? I'll open the gate for you."

I saw my words shock him, and I knew that until then he had not realized what he'd done. With the blood of the king's kin on his hands, he was outlawed, and no blood price could be paid. But he hesitated. "Gwenhwyfar—"

"Arthur still loves her, he'll protect her. It's her word against theirs now, and no evidence of anything. Go on, go!"

He got on the horse at last, and I ran for the gate, pulled the huge bars loose, and shoved the doors open. After he was through the gate and I heard his horse's hoofbeats dying away, I leaned against the wall and slid weakly to the ground, laughing with delight and relief.

The gamble had paid off; the dice had rolled in my favor. I was even glad I'd left witnesses alive behind me. I wanted there to be no doubt in Arthur's mind who had done this.

My father had thought—they'd all thought—that I would meekly accept being pushed aside, that I would be loyal and humble and grateful for being given much less than my due. But I had done what none of them had imagined possible: I'd split apart the power at the heart of Arthur's kingdom. Now Arthur would know the truth of me at last.

And what would become of Arthur's chosen heir? The neatness

with which I'd trapped my father in his own lies filled me with joy. How could Gwydre inherit the throne, when everyone would believe he was the son of a murderer?

Gwenhwyfach found me. She appeared so suddenly out of the shadows that I grabbed for my sword before I realized who it was. "Are you hurt?" She came to kneel beside me.

"No." I grinned up at her, catching my breath. "Are they all looking for him?"

"They'll be here in a minute. Medraud, what have you done? Gareth is dead. I thought you meant to catch them together and accuse them."

"Not enough. Arthur told me he'd never judge them guilty, no matter what the evidence." She didn't understand. She was frowning. "But this way Owain is fled, and his Ravens will go after him—Arthur's court is split down the middle, Gwen, and we did it!"

"Owain's fled?" she whispered. She looked up, shocked, at the open gate. "You'll start a war. Civil war, and the Saxons will come and take what's left over—"

"*I* will take what's left over!" I stared at her in dismay. "Don't be such a fool. What did you think I meant to do? You told me yourself, Gawain and the northern lords never loved Owain. Now that Owain has killed Gawain's brother, Arthur won't dare make peace with him. Without his pendragon he'll have no chance—"

"You didn't tell me. You never told me you meant to do this."

Something in her tone made me angry. I said sharply, "What promise have I made to tell you everything I know?" She moved her head as if I'd slapped her. It shouldn't have mattered—I didn't need her anymore—but I hated the way she was looking at me. "Come," I said, grabbing her hand and pulling her up as I got to my feet. "I have a boat waiting. We can't miss the tide. When we come back, would you like to be queen of Camelot? You can have Gwenhwyfar for your servant if you like."

"Civil war." She stood as still as Owain had, and I could hear voices behind her, coming from the hall. Her hand came up to touch her cheek, where the bruise still showed. "I thought you meant to shame her. I thought . . ." She shook her head. "How many more people have to die so you can make your father notice you?"

I twisted her hand in mine, turning down on the wrist so that it hurt. "Are you going to defend him too?" She didn't answer. "You think you'll betray me?"

"Was Gareth your enemy, Medraud? What had he done to you?"

"What do you care about him?" I could hear the voices growing louder. "He was stupid. He meant nothing. Gwen, don't—"

She didn't move. I glimpsed torchlight, heard the voices approaching. I let go of her hand and left her there.

20

I WENT TO IRELAND, OF COURSE—nowhere better to find troops to fight a British war. After some traveling I found a king's younger son, Rhiogan, whose warband was tired of kicking their heels between cattle raids. I told him about the treasures of Camelot: cattle, sheep, gold and jewelry, all the land a man could want, fine and fertile for crops. We hired as many warriors as we could afford, and then hired more with the promise of wealth to be had after the campaign was over: Irish and British, kings' sons and scarred old campaigners, landless men who needed any lord to follow.

Five months after I'd left my father's court, I stood together with Rhiogan on the plain below Camelot. A thin, cold rain was falling. All around the foot of Camelot's hill our forces were camped, just out of bow shot, waiting.

"Terrible weather, this." Rhiogan grumbled. He sneezed and rubbed his nose on the back of his hand. "The men are getting restless, Medraud. We've been here a month, already—how much longer do we have to wait?"

"Do you want to attack that, then?" Rhiogan shook his head,

staring up at Camelot's wall, stone to the height of a man and timber above that, with its towers for bowmen and its one massive gate. "Let them get restless; they'll fight all the better. Arthur will come out soon enough. He's not a fool, to wait until his army's half starved to try and break a siege."

"What if reinforcements come?"

"There's no way he could have gotten a messenger out. And who would he call on? None of the nearby kings have much of an army. It's peacetime, remember?"

"What about Owain Pendragon?"

I turned on him sharply. "Owain won't be back. I took care of him, I told you."

"You told me. But I've heard of the pendragon. He's pulled tricks before."

"He's a murderer here. He killed the king's own cousin! If Arthur made peace with Owain now, half his family would leave him to fight alone." Rhiogan's look of doubt infuriated me, but I kept my anger quiet; I needed him. "Don't worry. Owain won't be back. And Arthur won't stay inside much longer."

Rhiogan shrugged. "I hope not, then. We can't stay here all winter." He started back toward his tent. I pulled my cloak tighter around my shoulders and stood staring up at my father's city.

THAT NIGHT, as I was putting a fresh edge on my sword for lack of anything else to do, one of the men pushed aside the tent flap and stuck his head in. "Your pardon, lord, but there's a woman here says she must see you."

I looked up in surprise. There were women who had come with us from Ireland, and more had joined us as the siege went on, but they were generally not to my taste. "I don't want to see anyone."

"Yes sir, but she says—" A hand on his shoulder suddenly pushed him off balance, and Gwenhwyfach slipped past him into the tent. The guard grabbed her arm to pull her back.

"Let her go!" I said. "Leave us."

Gwenhwyfach had not moved or spoken. Her wet cloak dripped a circle of water on the trampled grass.

"Why are you here?" I demanded. "Did you think I'd take you back now?"

"I want to talk to you." I remembered the way her face had once glowed when she talked to me, as if the words were better than bread to her, sweeter than wine. There was nothing of that beauty in her now. "You used to listen to me."

"You used to be on my side. What do you want?"

"I want you to stop this."

"What?"

"Stop this." Her hand made a gesture toward the door of the tent, the walled city beyond. "It's your own brother you're fighting against. Your own father—"

"He's not my father!" Rage took my voice, and I had to breathe deeply to get it back again. Of all people, she should have known better than to say that to me. "Didn't he tell you? He's only my uncle, my mother's brother. And I have no brother; Gwydre is Owain's son."

"Medraud—"

"And what made you think I would stop just because you asked me?" I mocked her. "Do you think you mean that much to me?"

She pushed her cloak back on her shoulders. "I didn't think you would stop because I asked. But I thought you might . . ." Gently she smoothed the loose cloth of her dress against her sides, pulling it tight across her stomach. "It doesn't have anything to do with them, Medraud. With your father or your brother, or my sister. A child, yours and mine."

I shrugged. "How do I know it's mine?" Her hair seemed even darker against her suddenly pale face. "For all I know you've been sleeping with every man at the court. Maybe even the pendragon. Is that why you were so jealous of your sister? Maybe you even kept the king's bed warm for him while his wife entertained her lover."

"Shut up!" Her hand was on her knife, her face ugly with rage and shock and shame. "You know none of that is true—"

"I know nothing of the sort. You weren't a virgin when you came to my bed; how should I know how many others you've slept in?" I felt a sharp, sweet pleasure rising in me, the same way I'd felt when I'd faced Arthur at last. There is something intoxicating about the making of enemies, about burning your last bridges and seeing the flames dance in your opponent's eyes. "You chose to stay with Arthur. Go back and tell him I am his enemy forever."

She only stood there, saying nothing, until the look on her face made me angrier than ever. "Go on!" I shouted. "What are you waiting for? Get out!" I took a step toward her with my hand upraised, but she turned. I saw a last glimpse of her face, the white curve of her cheekbone under wet hair, the swirl of her cloak through the air.

THE RAIN DIED AWAY DURING THE NIGHT. When the dawn broke, the sky was cloudless, the air warmer than it had been in weeks. The grass of Camelot's hill glowed a brilliant green in the sun; the river curling around the foot of the north slope was a silver line, a white glaze of light.

Arthur attacked midmorning, his warriors on horseback pouring out of Camelot's gate. Our sentries had shouted a warning at the first sign of movement. I stumbled out of my tent, trying to buckle the chin strap of my helmet with one hand and adjust my sword belt with the other. Rhiogan, already armed and mounted, was shouting orders at the captains of the warbands, and our men were scrambling into position, just in time.

There was a moment when I stood still, nothing left to do, watching as Arthur's warriors gained momentum in their charge. His horses were all in the first rank. He meant to smash through our lines with their weight and speed, leaving us scattered and vulnerable. The dragon banner spread wide, glowing red in the sun. I thought I saw Arthur's helmet below it, the iron washed with bronze to shine like gold.

Our front line crouched in the grass, the men's shields up over their shoulders, waiting. The archers knelt behind them. The only sound was the thudding of the horses' hooves on the steep green slope, and I thought we would never hold them.

Then they were close enough. I heard the hum of a hundred bowstrings an instant before men and horses were screaming and dying.

Arthur's line didn't break, but it faltered. The men wore mail, but the horses did not, and warriors fell and rolled with their dying beasts. Rhiogan shouted the order to charge.

The noise was astonishing: the crash of metal on wood, the clang of metal on metal, men shouting their throats raw. I kept thinking of the battle with the sea raiders. Somehow the black confusion of that night seemed better suited to warfare than this bright, clear day. It was strange to see men bleeding and dying in broad daylight.

Behind our lines, on horseback, I watched as we pushed them, step by step, up the steep slope of Camelot's hill. The grass under the men's feet grew slippery with blood, and the smell of it in the hot sun was thick, salty, rotten, like spoiled meat.

I hung back, trying to see everything at once. Where was our line weakening? Where did we need more men? Hard to tell in the shifting mass of warriors which were ours, which Arthur's. It was the line of men in the center, shield to shield, struggling and shoving and dying that was crucial. I kept my eye on that, trying to shut out all distractions—the heat, the weight of my mail shirt, my growing thirst, the clamor of sword on sword, sword on shield. And the fact that I hadn't seen Arthur since that first charge.

Midway up Camelot's hill our slow advance ground to a halt. Arthur's force had reached a small plateau, and there they dug in their heels. Our men, still on the slope below them, could make little headway.

Rhiogan was shouting in my ear. I listened to him, then nodded. He wheeled off, calling for three of our warbands to follow him.

Now all we had to do was hold them. And we didn't. But we'd only lost a foot or so of ground when I saw black smoke and a few bright spots of flame along the wall to the south.

As we had known they would, three of Arthur's warbands ran

for the south, to protect the wall. Now, I thought, we should be able to make some progress. But we'd barely gained back the ground we'd lost when six more of Arthur's warbands were gone as well. But not to the south. They headed north, rounding the curve of Camelot's wall, and vanished before I could understand where or why. And what was left of Arthur's force scrambled in retreat to join the rearguard at the gate before they could be trampled by our men.

My warbands would have gone after them, and died charging at that heavily defended gate, if I hadn't yelled a halt. What was wrong? What was Arthur planning? He'd given us the hill when he could have made us pay for it inch by bloody inch.

The captains were all staring at me, waiting for my word. And I had no idea what to tell them.

"South," I snapped at last. "See if you can get that wall down." It might be easier to enter Camelot by tearing down the wall than hacking our way through the gate. And at any rate, it would keep the defending forces split. I just hoped, if we did manage to bring the wall down, that Rhiogan could keep our men on the battlefield and not looting in the city streets. "You"—I pointed at the leader of my own warband, a dark-haired, sullen and silent Irishman I'd chosen because he did whatever I told him without question—"you and your men come with me."

I kept a wary eye on the rearguard at the gate as we moved north, following the track of Arthur's warbands. We were vulnerable, but they'd have to leave the gate weakly defended to chase after us, and I was fairly sure they wouldn't dare.

We'd only gone a few hundred yards to the south when I saw movement, something bright against the green hills, like the flash of sunlight on metal. I squinted, swore, and moved my horse to one side to get a better view.

The river at the foot of Camelot's hill is impassable at high tide, but at low tide nearly a mile of it is shallow enough to be forded. The tide was ebbing now, and drawing near to the north bank was a host, perhaps three or four hundred strong. First I thought of Owain Pendragon, but then the wind caught the banner and spread it out: brown with a golden eagle, not Owain's black raven on a green ground. And most of the men were on foot, armed with spears; only a few were mounted. That smelled of Saxons to me.

On the south side of the river flew a banner I did know: the red dragon.

I signaled my men to follow me and kicked my horse to a gallop. I was shouting for Rhiogan before we were nearly close enough to him to hear.

21

HE WOODEN UPPER PORTION OF THE WALL was well and truly in flames by now, though the lower half, made of stone, stood firm. The black smoke spread like fog through the bright, clean air; I could feel the heat even well back from the flames. The fight was a mess, the lines broken and scattered, hard to tell enemies from allies. Arthur's men must be the tight knot with their backs to the fire, struggling to keep our men from breaking through. But we had them outnumbered, and more of them fell even as I watched. Without reinforcements they couldn't last long.

I spotted Rhiogan's white horse, heard him yelling furiously, trying to restore some order to the lines. I shouted to get his attention, waving him over.

We both dismounted, keeping a tight grasp on the horses' reins. My warband surrounded us so we could talk without worrying about the enemy. "What's Arthur planning?" Rhiogan demanded. "The men say he pulled off half his force!"

"Listen!" I had to raise my voice to be heard over the growl and hiss of the flames, the clamor of the battle. "There's a Saxon warband across the river—Arthur's down there trying to hold the ford against them!"

"Saxons?" His teeth were white against skin dark gray with smoke and sweat and ash. "The gods are with us! We'll pull back and let them fight each other, and whoever wins will still have us to deal with!"

"No! We have to get down there. Arthur can't hold that ford alone—"

"Did you get hit in the head sometime in all this?" Rhiogan gaped at me. "Are you mad? The Saxons will do our work for us!"

"This is *my* war," I told him, my voice low enough to undercut the tumult around us. "You will do as I tell you. Get your men down to the ford, now."

"I will do nothing of the sort—"

I hit him, a backhanded slap that knocked him sprawling. He started to scramble up with a hand to his sword, but I had my blade out and at his throat. The men around us stood frozen, but they were loyal to me first; they wouldn't intervene.

"I am in command here," I reminded my ally. "Pull your men off the wall and get them down to the ford." I sheathed my sword. Leaving Rhiogan staring after me, I pulled my warband together and rode for the ford, determined that no one should kill my father but myself.

We rounded the curve of Camelot's wall just in time to see the first Saxons gaining the south shore of the river. I signaled to my men to split and sweep around on either side of Arthur's warband. As we crashed into the Saxon force, I saw Arthur raise his sword in a great sweeping stroke and bring it down.

The light began to fade as we drove them back across the river. There would be no more hanging back, no more directing the fighting from behind the lines. Now we needed every sword.

I was glad. My hand had itched for my sword hilt all day. To stand back and watch other men fighting my war—that was not what I'd spent all those years training for.

Anyone trying to scramble up the slick, muddy riverbank was an enemy. The fighting was close; men were on either side of me, grabbing at my horse's bridle and dodging to avoid his hooves. I knocked spears aside and looked for Arthur. I didn't see him. Men went down under my horse's hooves, under my sword. I saw the captain of my warband fall, an arrow in his throat. He sprawled in the water, and his flowing blood unraveled in the current.

My sword arm ached; my throat burned with tiredness. Blood dripped down my leg from a cut along my thigh. After a while I saw that the water had risen, above my horse's knees, touching my boots. The tide was turning, and soon the river would be too deep to ford.

The fighting had spread out, and for the moment I was alone. I turned my horse back to our side of the river. As he struggled up the bank, two Saxons were on me, clawing at my shield arm, trying to drag me from the saddle. I landed a blow and one of them fell, a great slash through his neck, but the other hooked a hand in my belt and pulled me down on top of him.

I lost my sword and shield in the impact, and he his spear, but he still had a knife. Clutching at each other's hands, we rolled together over the ground. I ended up flat on my back, the Saxon a suffocating weight on top of me. I could feel his sour breath on my face, hear him panting in my ear.

Both of his hands and one of mine were on his knife. He was stronger than I was. No matter how I hard I tried to lock my elbow, his weight bent my arm slowly but steadily, the knife coming closer and closer to my throat.

With my free hand I groped down for the dagger at my belt. I couldn't find it. Had it gone in the fall too? The point of his blade brushed my skin, and at last I touched the hilt of my own knife. It was awkward to draw it with my left hand; my gloved fingers slipped on the polished hilt. I felt blood dripping warm down my neck as I pulled the knife free. With a quick thrust I buried the blade deep between his ribs.

I watched his blue eyes go wide and glazed with the shock and I kicked him off me, scrambling to my feet and snatching up my sword and shield. My horse had bolted.

The last glowing sliver of the sun slid beneath the trees to the west as I looked over the battlefield. A gray mist was closing in, erasing the line of the trees against the sky. I touched a hand to my neck, but the cut wasn't deep; the flow of blood slowed to a trickle. There was no one nearby, and I risked kneeling down beside the river to scoop up a handful of dirty water and hold it to my lips. It tasted of earth and my own sweat.

There was a dead man lying face up in the mud beside me. His gray eyes were wide open and he looked somehow familiar. I studied him for a moment before I recognized Rhiogan's face.

I looked up quickly and saw Arthur.

He was unhorsed like I was, fighting on the ground by the river's edge, near a small grove of willows. The men around him were weakening before an onslaught of Saxons. Arthur's helmet gleamed gold in the last of the light. In a minute they would have him. In a minute my father would be dead.

I gripped my sword and ran toward him.

Arthur was tiring as I reached him, his sword rising too slowly to parry at his opponent's stroke. I brought my blade down on his attacker's wrist, and the man dropped his sword with a scream and a shower of blood. I slammed my shield into another man's face, breaking his nose and sending him sprawling. Dropping the shield, I grabbed Arthur with my free hand and shoved him backward, knocking him to the ground. I spun around to stand over him, my bad leg nearly buckling under me, swinging my sword in wide, two-handed arcs that kept his attackers at bay.

For the space of a few heartbeats. Then a spear got under my guard; my mail shirt turned the thrust, but it still doubled me over, sending me to my knees. It probably saved my life as well, for a sword swung over my head as I dropped. I heard Arthur yelling behind me.

Looking up, blinking my eyes clear, I saw more of Arthur's men around us. The Saxons ran or were cut down. Someone grabbed hold of my sword arm, but I was still too busy trying to breathe to do anything about it.

"I said leave him be!" Arthur's voice, furious. The hand let go of my arm. Arthur was on his knees beside me, his arm around my shoulders. "Medraud. Medraud, are you hurt?" I shook my head. In a few minutes, I could breathe without feeling like I was swallowing coals. I sat up. Over our heads, the branches of three tall willows were intertwined; the tips of their long leaves brushed the ground on either side. Arthur's men—only five of them left standing—surrounded us, staring in blank astonishment. Impatiently Arthur waved them back a few paces.

My father and I sat looking at each other. After a while I asked the only question I could think of. "Where's Gwydre?"

Arthur sat back on his heels. Beneath his helmet, astonishment, relief, exasperation played on his face. "He's not here. I sent him up north, for safety."

I thought of how Gwenhwyfach had tried to dissuade me, telling me I would be fighting my own brother. Well, I was hardly one to condemn anyone for lying.

"He wouldn't be much use on the battlefield anyway," Arthur said regretfully. "I should have let him be a silversmith long ago, and stopped trying to turn him into a king."

It was strange, hearing words from the whispers and rumors I'd worked so hard to spread coming from Arthur. It made me dizzy for a moment, wondering which of us was speaking.

"Medraud," Arthur said. "You came to fight a war against me, and you just saved my life. I don't know what to say to you."

My father, bewildered. There was a strange satisfaction in that. At last he knew that he'd never understood me. And he would never understand that, for the few moments when his life had depended on me, I'd gotten what I wanted: the fate of his kingdom in my hands.

"Medraud," Arthur persisted. "Can't you tell me why, at least?" I shook my head. Gwenhwyfach's voice, faint but so clear I almost thought she must be standing next to me: *"How many more people have to die?"* I was too tired to speak. Wedging the point of my sword into the ground before me, I pulled myself up with both hands on the hilt. A terrible way to use a good blade, but at least it got me upright. Arthur got to his feet as well.

The fighting seemed to be dying down; only isolated groups of men still struggled here and there. On the other side of the river, what was left of the Saxon army was trying to regroup—for retreat, I hoped, not another battle in the morning. It was growing darker.

"Medraud," Arthur insisted. I turned wearily to him, and

watched with a distant interest as the expression of tenderness and confusion on his face turned to alarm. He was staring over my shoulder at the trees behind me. "Medraud, look—"

I turned just in time to see the spear, thrown from close in and with such force that it cut through my mail shirt, already weakened by the previous blow. The sharp point sank deep into my side just below the ribs.

None of us had seen the Saxons, three of them, before they came at us from behind the trees. Trapped on our side of the river by the rising tide, they'd apparently decided to die boldly rather than wait for capture—and to take some of their enemies with them as well.

As I sprawled on the ground, unable to breathe, Arthur stayed on his knees beside me, shouting orders to his men.

They charged the Saxons, but I had been wrong, there were more than three, hidden in the shadows under the trees. I saw Arthur's warriors fall: Gereint, clutching with both hands at the blood that poured from his throat; Hafgan, stumbling, blind, his helmet gone, his face a red mask.

Arthur stood over me, his sword in his hand. Protecting me? After I had betrayed him, waged war on him, brought his kingdom down around his head in ruins? I wanted to tell him to run. He still had a chance to escape; his men were dying to give it to him. But there was no air in my lungs to form words, to warn him of the warrior I saw behind him, the sword rising. Then my father fell on top of me, and as he fell, I saw his eyes and mouth wide with shock, and blood flying in an arc from the back of his head.

The Saxon bent down and heaved Arthur roughly off me. He stood looking down at me, grinning, while his sword swung up for the final blow. I stared up at him, tall, light-haired as Gwydre, blood striping his cheek.

The sword balanced for a moment at the top of its swing, plain dark iron, short and heavy and deadly. My own sword was too far away, but Arthur's lay just beside me. I seized it, and clenched my left hand around the wooden shaft of the spear, slick with my own blood, and used it to pull myself up. As the Saxon's sword came down, I thrust the blade into his stomach with all my strength, sliding it up underneath his ribs. His stroke continued, but missed, as I fell back down. He dropped the sword, staggered a few steps away, and fell.

Whimpering, I took hold of the spear shaft again and pulled the iron head free of my flesh. The point wasn't barbed, and came out easily. The rush of blood was scalding hot. I lay there panting a few minutes, and then crawled to Arthur's side.

I unbuckled the strap under his chin and carefully pulled his helmet off. The Saxon's sword had struck the back of his head, just under the edge of the helmet. His dark eyes were open and unfocused. I leaned closer, whispered his name; I could feel his breath against my cheek. His lips moved, but no sound came out.

Painfully, I tugged Arthur's body close to the nearest tree, cushioning his head as much as I could. Every time I breathed I tasted blood in my mouth. At last I rested with my back against the tree trunk and laid Arthur's head on my lap. One look at his wound had shown me that the bone was crushed. There was nothing to be done.

Arthur didn't move again. Nor did anybody else. Behind me, I could hear a faint moaning, shattered and broken. As I stayed still, listening, it stopped.

My father and I waited there together, among the bodies of his men and his enemies, while it grew darker and the mist rolled slowly up from the riverbed. Across the river I heard the Saxons gather the remains of their forces and retreat.

Arthur whispered my name. I leaned down to hear his words, slurred and faint. "Medraud—ask whatever you want, and I will give it. You saved my life."

Always the king, doling out gifts to his loyal followers. Didn't he know that wasn't what I wanted from him? But then I thought of Gwenhwyfach, her dark eyes, her strong hands curved around her belly, to support and protect. "Gwenhwyfach carries my child," I said slowly. "Let our child be your heir."

Arthur's eyelids flickered in acknowledgement. "A witness." I could barely hear him. "We need a witness."

I looked out. In the fading light, a few stumbling figures still moved on the battlefield. I tried to call, but what started as a shout came out of my lips barely a whisper. At last I managed it, not loud, but in the silence of an empty battlefield it was enough.

One of the men, near our tree, stopped and came warily toward us, his sword before him. "Who's there?" he called. I recognized him: one of Arthur's warriors, Bedwyr. He came closer, squinting, and saw us.

"Arthur!" He fell on his knees beside us, glanced vaguely at me, and returned his gaze to his king's face. "Arthur, oh, my lord . . ." Bedwyr had grown sons, but his voice in exhaustion and grief was as wavering and tear-filled as a boy's.

Arthur raised a shaking hand to still him. "I call you to witness," he said faintly, his voice rasping over the formal words. "I choose as my heir the child, son or daughter, of my son Medraud and Gwenhwyfach, half sister to the queen." He closed his eyes, braced himself, and opened them to meet Bedwyr's gaze. "Witness it!" he whispered fiercely.

"I—I hear and witness," Bedwyr choked out.

"My sword," Arthur commanded. Bedwyr looked around in bewilderment, found the blade, and brought it to Arthur's side. "Take it to the queen and tell her what you have witnessed." With a sigh Arthur lay back, his eyes closed.

"My lord," Bedwyr protested. "I will take you to Camelot; the healers can look at your wound."

"No," Arthur whispered. "I will stay with my son."

Did it take all this, I thought, *to make you say that to me?* "Go on," I snarled at Bedwyr. "You heard what he said—leave us!" The soldier stumbled to his feet and backed away. I thought I heard him crying.

IT HAS GROWN DARK SINCE THEN, and cold. The only warmth is my blood flowing against my side.

Arthur hasn't moved or spoken since Bedwyr left us. I don't think he's breathing. I want to close his eyes, pale in the darkness, looking up at me. But my hand has gotten too heavy to lift from where it lies on the earth at my side.

But then Arthur stirs, his head moving a little, his eyes flickering as though he's seen something in the gloom. "Morgan?" he whispers, the word no louder than a breath. "Love . . ." His voice fades, his eyes fall shut.

Looking up, I see a woman just a few feet away. She could have been carved from mist and darkness and moonlight, she stands so quietly. But it isn't my mother. It's Gwenhwyfach.

At last she comes and kneels down beside us. She takes my hand. I can feel her fingers around my own, hot with the living blood that pulses through them.

It takes me a while to find my voice. "Our child will be Arthur's heir," I tell her.

Her face is distant. I cannot see her eyes.